# The room was
# dark and warm . . .

and when he wrapped his arms around her, she fell into the depths of all that he was offering her. His breath was uneven and ragged, and his hand slid down the front of her sweater. "You feel so good. I can't believe you're here with me."

Her eyes closed as his finger stroked over her breast. She felt the sweater glide up over her bare skin. "I'm here."

"Good," he whispered. His lips moved like the sea over her throat and onto her shoulder, and in one powerful motion, he pulled her up into the juncture of his body.

Adam had thought of this moment. He had dreamed it, and the dream had washed away the loneliness. He couldn't let her go. He needed the dream to be real. Just for the night.

He carried her to the bed and came down over her, fully clothed, moving against her, prolonging the sweet agony. "This is where I've dreamed about you, Erica."

She pressed against him. "I'm not a dream, Adam. I'm real."

# ABOUT THE AUTHOR

A native of Oklahoma, Andrea Davidson graduated from the University of Missouri and began her writing career with the American Medical Association in Chicago. After free-lancing for medical journals and magazines after the birth of her children, she turned to romance writing. Andrea now lives on a ranch in Texas with her husband, son and daughter.

## Books by Andrea Davidson

### HARLEQUIN AMERICAN ROMANCE

1—THE GOLDEN CAGE
16—MUSIC IN THE NIGHT
21—UNTAMED POSSESSION
45—TREASURES OF THE HEART
122—AN UNEXPECTED GIFT
324—THE BEST GIFT OF ALL

### HARLEQUIN INTRIGUE

25—A SIREN'S LURE
41—OUT FROM THE SHADOWS

Don't miss any of our special offers. Write to us at the following address for information on our newest releases.

Harlequin Reader Service
901 Fuhrmann Blvd., P.O. Box 1397, Buffalo, NY 14240
Canadian address: P.O. Box 603,
Fort Erie, Ont. L2A 5X3

# ANDREA DAVIDSON

## THE LIGHT ON WILLOW LANE

# *Harlequin Books*

TORONTO • NEW YORK • LONDON
AMSTERDAM • PARIS • SYDNEY • HAMBURG
STOCKHOLM • ATHENS • TOKYO • MILAN

"She would rather light candles than curse the darkness, and her glow has warmed the world."
—Adlai E. Stevenson
(about Eleanor Roosevelt)

Published December 1990

ISBN 0-373-16371-1

# Prologue

The water was smooth as glass, and the boat skimmed like a lazy gull over its surface. He felt nothing but that silky smoothness, like the feel of a satin nightgown, like a hand gliding up a soft thigh. A horn honked outside the bedroom window, but the sound didn't reach him. He was gliding, gliding across an endless calm expanse of nothingness.

And then it came. Suddenly. Inexplicably. A hand, fisted and huge—a boxer's hand, swinging in a wide arc—shot across the water. The blow caught him by surprise. A line of demarcation had been drawn, one he was not supposed to cross. He tried not to. He tried to hold himself back and dodge that powerful and malevolent force. But it was too strong. He felt the boat listing. The water parted. He was pulled down, drawn into a hopeless battle that had no reason, into a nether world of rage without basis. He knew, in the few seconds before it happened, that he was going to be swallowed by the boiling chasm. Something ugly came at him from down below the surface. It rose upward and fell over him, crushing him, pulling him down. From the depths of his tormented mind, he heard a woman cry out his name. He heard a child's *pitiful scream. Hot tongues of fire licked at his body. He prayed that the water would wash over him and drown him, but the fire burned through his flesh, through his bones, and he cried out in pain.*

"Daddy?"

Adam threw back the covers and stared vacantly at the small thing in a blue cotton nightgown. He heard, as if from some far-off place, the sleepy voice calling him daddy, but he couldn't acknowledge her. He didn't even recognize her. When he finally did, he became aware of the tears that rolled down his cheeks and, mingling with the cold sweat from his body, soaked the pillow and sheets beneath him.

He forced himself upright, swung his legs over the side of the bed and planted his feet on the floor. With trembling fingers, he reached for a glass of water beside the bed and drank it.

"It's okay," he finally managed, but his voice cracked with the lie.

"You called for us again," said the small wavering voice.

He wiped his hand across his face and strove for a full breath of air. "I'm sorry I woke you."

"Did you have another bad dream?"

He tried to focus on her, but the night and the hot liquid behind his eyes made it difficult. It took all his effort to find his voice, and when he did it was scratchy and raw. "Yes. A—a bad dream. But it's okay now. I...why don't you go back to bed. Okay?" he added, aware of the sound of pleading in his own voice.

"Okay." Tiny feet carried the blue cotton nightgown across the room. The little girl stopped in the open doorway. "I'll leave the light in the hall on, Daddy. Just in case you get scared again."

Outside his window, the other houses on Willow Lane were delineated with rows of Christmas bulbs in red, green, blue and yellow, a painful reminder of a month Adam wanted to erase from his mind forever. He listened to Jilly's feet padding down the hallway, and he watched as the hall light came on. Smothering an anguished cry, he buried his face in his hands and wept.

# Chapter One

*A world of dreams. Beautiful dreams and fantasies.* That's what life had been like for Erica Manning. Everyone said so. Everyone believed it. Even Erica had convinced herself that it was, indeed, true.

She had always been the first and the best and the prettiest. All the contests, all the laurels, all the titles had been hers. Little Miss Toddler at two. Little City Princess at five. Miss Teen... Miss Southern Deb... Miss City... County... State. Only the big one, the crème de la crème, had escaped her grasp. She had been declared runner-up to Miss America, and the humiliation had almost destroyed her. Because, for the first time in her life, she had come in second best.

If she ever pried open the door to peer at the past and examine herself closely, she would remember that she had been thrilled to make it that far. Thrilled, that is, until her father's bitter disappointment and embarrassment had stamped out any sense of triumph. It was in his projection that she saw herself as second-best. In his way of thinking, it was less than zero. A loser.

Since that time, her life had been a series of steps to prove herself worthy in his eyes, in everyone's eyes.

She wanted desperately to believe that she was almost there.

Erica surveyed the clear warm day outside the restaurant window. Strings of Christmas lights dangled above the intersections, and the display windows in the shop across the street were alive with robotic elves, simulated snow and live mannequins in parkas. It was almost perfect.

She took a sip of Earl Grey tea and frowned. "Why doesn't it snow?"

Parker Manning II looked up from his brunch menu and across the table at his daughter. "People who want snow live north of the Mason-Dixon."

"I know, I know, but it's just not Christmas."

He drank some of his Bloody Mary. "All in the mind, my dear. All in the mind. Although, I too have to admit that this isn't exactly Currier and Ives."

Erica heard the low hum of the air conditioner come on in the restaurant, and she groaned, "Hardly. Here it is the first week of December and it's eighty degrees. Can you believe it?"

"Cheer up. At least we're not buried to our eyeballs in snow and ice."

*Cheer up?* She wasn't sure she knew the meaning of the words. This was supposed to be the season of cheer, happiness and glad tidings. She began to drum her nails against the cream linen tablecloth. There wasn't time to cheer up. There really wasn't time for Christmas. There wasn't time for anything except clawing and scratching her way to glory in the next battle.

Oh, but she was so tired. If only...if only...

She didn't even know what it was she sought. She knew only that something was lacking in her life. But how could that be? For what had Erica ever needed that she hadn't been given?

Her gloomy thoughts were interrupted when a friend of her father's stopped by the table. After greeting them both, he turned to Erica and smiled. "I watched your new television program the other day, honey. You were sensational."

Her smile was gracious, as always, and her tone was self-assured. "Thank you."

"Isn't she great!" Parker said, beaming. "That station was damned lucky to get someone of my daughter's caliber. Took them long enough to come to their senses and give her her own program."

"So you'll be hosting the *Focal Point* show from now on?" the man asked.

"Well—" Erica's gaze flickered briefly to her father "—not exactly. There are three of us right now. We have a sort of unofficial competition going on, I guess you'd say." Erica smiled at the man and refused to acknowledge her father's stony countenance.

"Well, that's great, honey," he said, smiling at Parker and giving Erica a token pat on the shoulder. *Isn't that cute,* he might just as easily have said.

When he was gone, she chanced a look at her father. His expression was granite. "Why did you tell him that?" he said in a low, hard voice.

"What?"

"That you are in competition with those other two. Why didn't you just say you were the new host?"

"Because it would have been a lie."

His disdain landed like a rock in the pit of her stomach. "Then you'd better learn to lie," he said. "Hell, Erica, I thought I'd taught you better than that. You're never to let your opponent know what hand you're holding.''

''He wasn't an opponent, Dad. He was some—some friend of yours.''

''He's not a friend.''

''Okay, acquaintance then. And this isn't a poker game.''

''All of life is a poker game. You either win the hand or you don't.'' He shook his head. ''What the hell has happened to you?''

''Good grief, Dad.'' She laughed nervously. ''Nothing has happened to me. Anyway,'' she added, hoping to soothe over any ill feelings that might be brewing between them, ''I *am* trying to secure the position. It's just that nothing has been decided yet.''

He scoffed at that. ''It's in the bag for you, Princess. Who else deserves it? Those other two don't stand a chance against you. Believe me, I've seen what they look like.''

''Looks aren't what count here, Dad. Brains are. Journalistic savvy.''

''Hogwash. Your looks have taken you this far. That's all the audience cares about anyway.''

Erica took a stab at her fruit and silently hoped that her father was wrong. Looks were important in television journalism, sure. But they weren't everything. Were they?

''I haven't been able to come up with a meaty enough topic. That's the problem. Manda had that kindergarten child abuse case on Tuesday. Karen covered the collapse of Standard Savings and Loan yesterday.'' Erica tapped her fork on the edge of the plate. ''My last program was on that trainer who was mauled at the zoo.''

"You worry too much. I'm telling you, they won't even consider the other two. It's in the cards for you."

Her father, the gambler, had always put high stakes on her. And, doing her part, she always came through with a winning hand. That had been her role in life, and she had played it without questioning why.

The waiter set down plates of eggs Benedict. Erica really wasn't all that hungry, but she made an effort to enjoy it.

"You know," she said, looking out the window, "what I'd really like to do is something on that Tobias case. Now that would be a prime topic."

"Why is that?"

"Well, with the acquittal of the boy last week, it's hot. Emotions are at fever pitch over the jury's decision."

"There just wasn't enough evidence to convict him," said Parker, shrugging.

Erica's forehead creased, and she stared out the window. "There might have been if his parents had told what they knew."

"They were just protecting him."

"But did they have that right?"

Parker shrugged again. "I'd do the same for you, Princess."

She stared at him. "Even if I were charged with murder?"

He stared back. "Even if."

She looked away. "I still think there's a story in there somewhere."

"So, if that's what you want, why don't you do it?"

"I contacted the law firm, the one that represented Mr. and Mrs. Tobias. The attorney who handled it— what was his name?—Adams, I think, no Adam.

That's it, Adam Bech." She shook her head. "The man wouldn't even give me the time of day."

"How did you approach him?"

"Well, I called him, told him who I was and that I wanted to interview him for the *Focal Point* show." She smirked. "He wasn't impressed."

"That's because he didn't see you. You should have gone to his office and met him face-to-face. One look and he wouldn't have been able to resist."

"He didn't sound that easy, Dad. I don't know— there was something about his voice...."

"What?"

Erica stared out the window. How could she explain to her father that a voice over the telephone could affect her the way Adam Bech's had? Sexy and powerful and, despite her father's assurance, totally unsusceptible to anyone's charm—hers included. "He just sounded—well, definite."

"I know the senior partner in that firm," said Parker. "Dub Grobinski."

"Really? How well do you know him?"

Parker took a bite of egg and chewed mechanically. "Well enough. Let's just say the man is indebted to me."

How easy it would be right now to ask her father for help, knowing full well that if she asked, it would be done. It had always been that way between them. If she wanted something and, if it would further both of their goals, then it was hers.

But she had reached the point in her life when she wanted to make it on her own. She had depended on him for so many years and had let him control her every move and thought. She knew it was high time she was doing for herself. Still . . .

"Can you get him for me, Dad?" she asked tentatively, hating herself for accepting the easy way out once again.

"Of course I'll speak to him."

"And you think that he'll agree to do the show or have Adam Bech do it?"

Parker Manning smiled at his beautiful daughter and reached for her hand. "I've told you a hundred times, Princess, whatever you want is yours. You just have to go after it. If you want this lawyer to do your show, then he's yours. If you want the show to be all yours, then it's yours. All you have to do is want to win. And you have to admit that winning is everything. That's where your edge comes in." His eyes narrowed on his daughter's face. "You do want to win, Erica. Don't you?"

Erica glanced out the window at the warm, dry day and knew that what she wanted more than anything right now was for it to feel like Christmas. But it just didn't.

She turned back to her father—the man who wanted her to win, who wanted and expected her to be perfect in every way—and said, "Of course I do, Dad. I want to win. What else is there?"

FOLLOWING THROUGH on his promise, her father called Dub Grobinski and secured his permission to interview Adam Bech. That afternoon Erica drove over to the law offices.

The secretary announced her but, after hearing her boss's unenthusiastic response, she hesitated before leading Erica into Mr. Bech's office.

Adam Bech leaned back in his big leather chair, one ankle resting across his knee, his hands hooked behind his neck—a study in relaxed confidence. But it was the eyes that immediately gave him away. Erica had seen that look many times. He was poised for confrontation, expecting the worst, ready to attack head-on. This man was neither relaxed nor happy.

She stood for a moment in the doorway, taking in the room and its occupant. The voice on the phone, she now realized, had conjured up an accurate picture. He was incredibly handsome, with dark brown hair and gray-washed eyes that watched her every move, missing nothing.

She took a deep breath to steady her pulse. She had been around handsome men all her life. And she had faced confrontation in interviews before. This was simply another step in the forward march. There was absolutely no justification for the sudden rise in her pulse rate.

"Thank you for taking the time to see me, Mr. Bech."

Her voice was soft and feminine, an appealing sound that immediately put him on the defensive. "I'm doing this as a favor—"

"I appreciate that, then."

"To my partner," he added pointedly.

"Oh." Erica stared at the man across the large paneled office. A far cry from her own nine-by-nine cubicle, this room spelled success. It was the workplace of a man who had made it to the top of his profession.

She suddenly felt like a schoolgirl who had been called before the principal. She didn't like the feeling one little bit.

The leather creaked as he shifted in his chair. Signaling for her to sit in the chair opposite the desk, he planted both feet on the floor, scooted into the desk and rested his forearms on the table, hoping to appear more collected and businesslike than he felt.

Voices on the telephone, he knew, could be deceiving, so when she had called yesterday, he had forced himself to stay immune to the soft, lilting voice. But now that he saw her face-to-face, he realized there was much more than just a voice to which he would have to remain immune. Her eyes were a pale blue, giving her a deceptively guileless look. And with that halo of blond hair swirling free, angelic was the thought that first came to mind, a thought that was quickly discarded when he remembered how he had been coerced into this interview.

His voice was gruff in retaliation. "I don't watch daytime television, Miss Manning, so maybe you should tell me what it is you're after. I'm not familiar with—what is the name of the program?"

*"Focal Point."*

He pulled a legal-sized yellow pad over in front of him and began to doodle on it. It gave him something to do other than look at her, but it really irked him that he felt the need *not* to look at her. "Right. *Focal Point.*"

"It's a general-interest program where we highlight various subjects."

He drew a few squiggly lines on the pad and then stopped, reluctantly raising his eyes. "Why me, Miss Manning? Why this story? Surely there are other issues more interesting to your viewers."

She noticed a tiny hint of something besides gruffness in his voice, something akin to panic. Was Adam Bech afraid? And, if so, of what? Surely not of her. Certain men had always been nervous around her, but this man didn't seem the type. And it wasn't uncommon for people to feel jittery about being on television, but somehow she didn't think that was what troubled him, either. There was something else and it intrigued her.

"It is a fascinating story, Mr. Bech. Here's a boy on trial for murder and, when the state calls his parents as its prime witness, they refuse, claiming their religion gives them basis for such a refusal. Now, I don't know, Mr. Bech, but I find that fascinating."

*Beautiful* was a word that came easily to mind as he looked at Erica Manning, although the assessment, he sternly reminded himself, was followed by no emotional or physical response. It was merely that—an assessment, something he could do from a remote psychological distance. In the past year that was the way he had responded to most people, coolly, detached, with total objectivity. A wall had come up between himself and the rest of the world and, while he knew it was there, he had no intention or desire to tear it down.

And now, here he was sitting across from one of the most beautiful women he had seen in a long time, feeling nothing but a kind of frosty animosity. All he wanted to do was to get this over with so he could go back to work.

"There have been other such cases," he said, hoping that fact alone would make her lose interest. "It's not unique."

"Maybe you can give me the names of some of these other cases. It might help with my research."

"I suppose," he answered reluctantly. "But I'm not really sure what it is you want out of this interview."

All of her life, men had made a fuss over her. Erica had always been the darling of her father's set. She had wowed the judges all the way to the top. And she had landed a job with the television station on the first interview. But in the past couple of years she had learned the hard way that something more was expected of her than just a pretty smile and a string of beauty titles.

It was obvious she wasn't going to win this man's cooperation with looks alone. This one would demand much more. "What I'm looking for, Mr. Bech, is a clear explanation about this case. It may not be unique, but it is unusual, and I want to devote the entire program to it. That would be approximately an hour and ten minutes. The show runs an hour and a half, but we've got to leave time for the news and sponsors."

"Is this to be live or taped?"

"Taped. And it will probably take several sessions to do the complete taping."

Adam impatiently tapped his pen on the desk. "How many is several, Miss Manning?"

"Two, maybe three."

"That's a big chunk of my time."

"And mine, Mr. Bech."

He sniffed. "Hardly the same thing. You and your show benefit from this little arrangement."

The smile she confronted him with was a cross between impish and beguiling. "Well, now that all depends, Mr. Bech."

"On what?"

"On how well you do in the interview."

Adam pursed his lips and studied her closely, holding back the smile that wanted to spontaneously erupt.

He wasn't about to let himself give in to the temptation. "Is this the way you get all of your interviews, Miss Manning?"

She cocked her head. "What do you mean?"

"I mean do you always have your father set them up for you?"

Although she heard a hint of teasing in his voice, Erica blanched. "That's unfair, Mr. Bech. We all use contacts. I'm sure you've called in your share of chips in the past."

"When it was expedient."

"Well, this is for me."

"Why?"

This was not going the way she had planned, at all. She wasn't about to discuss her career with a stranger, especially with someone she was trying to capture for the show. So why, then, did she have no control over the words that poured out of her mouth? "I have to do this, Mr. Bech. I'm in a highly aggressive competition for the host position on the show. I need a story like this one. I need something to give me an edge. This is very important to me. I could really use your help."

Her breath came out in a loud whoosh, and her eyes closed briefly while she cringed inside. Oh, God, why on earth had she said that? What an idiot he must think she was! What a total—

"Why didn't you tell me that on the phone yesterday?"

She opened her eyes and stared at him. His voice was very different now, less confrontational. "Well, I—uh—"

"When do we begin taping?"

She hoped her mouth wasn't hanging open, but the abrupt change in him was so unexpected. "Next week.

But we probably need to get together before that to go over the content a bit.''

"All right, when?"

"What is your schedule like this week?"

He flipped through his calendar, seeing none of the scribbled notations that would fill the next few days. He was aware only of the blind idiocy of what he was about to suggest. "Maybe we could meet for dinner Thursday night."

She tried to hide her surprise and pleasure, but it came across in her smile. "I'd love to. Should I meet you here after work?"

His throat felt constricted, his pulse pounded. Aware of the mistake he had just made but unable to counter it, he nodded like a puppet. "That'll be fine."

IT WAS ANYTHING BUT FINE. Ever since she had left his office, he'd been saying the same thing. *It was anything but fine.* It was terrible!

Adam turned his moody gaze from the purple sunset through the window, his eyes seeking out something to divert his thoughts. He stared at his partner's head. That was a diversion. It was an amusing head, shaped like the earth, an oblate spheroid, an egg. And like the earth, it was a tableau of multihued patches, ridges, trenches and bumps. Down low, along the tropic of Capricorn, was a band of wispy gray hair that curved up and around the base of his skull like a halo gone slightly askew. It was not a pretty head, but it and the man drew the admiration and envy of many. Adam included.

"It was a mistake," Adam murmured.

Dub Grobinski closed the file in his lap and looked up. "What was?"

Adam knew he couldn't tell Dub that he'd invited a beautiful woman to have dinner with him. Dub would smile and tell him how glad he was for him, making Adam feel even more miserable than he already did. "I hate talk shows," he said in way of explanation. "I'll be lousy."

"Nonsense. I'm glad you decided to do it."

"Why?"

Dub shrugged. "It's a tough issue. Maybe an explanation wouldn't hurt." He shook his head and smiled ruefully. "That's not entirely it. The truth is, I owe Parker Manning."

Dub Grobinski owed Parker Manning? That one baffled Adam. He couldn't imagine Dub owing anybody anything. Dub was one of the most talented defense lawyers in the country. Several years before, a creative journalist had named him the Nemean lion because of his tough-skinned approach in the courtroom, and the nickname had stuck. Any prosecutor who had the misfortune to come up against Dub Grobinski knew it would take a Herculean effort to make it through the trial with reputation intact, much less with victory in hand.

No, it was the world who owed Dub. *And I, too,* thought Adam as he looked at the older partner, his large bulk relaxed in the sumptuous leather chair. A class act, thought Adam, that's what this office was. It was one of the things that had always exhilarated him about working here, one of the things that had drawn him to the firm in the first place. It had a name, it had a brilliant staff. But most of all it had class, a quality that, to a young man from the mesquite-dotted dust bowl of West Texas, had been as compelling and as irresistible as the Holy Grail. Dub had made it possible for the fantasy to become a reality.

"And it is his daughter's show," Dub was saying. "But, of course, you met her this afternoon."

Met her and invited her for a date, Adam thought miserably. How could he have been so stupid? It was those eyes or that soft voice or... It was temporary insanity, that's what it was!

"I'd go on the program," Dub told Adam. "But I've got these series of depositions and then this grand jury hearing coming up."

Adam groaned and raised his hand. "I know, I'm going to do it. I'm just not thrilled about it, that's all."

Dub inhaled lovingly on a cigar he was forbidden to smoke at home and chuckled. "Oh, come on, Adam, you're a charmer. Always have been. My only hesitation in having you do it is that I don't want to pay overtime to the secretaries who'll have to deal with all the fan mail you're going to get." He laughed. "Yep, you'll have women panting on the sidewalk below and waiting on our doorstep every morning."

It was like a sudden flash of lightning the way it struck Adam. Here he was carrying on lightly with Dub as if nothing had happened to either of them, as if a foundation still supported them, as if their lives still had roots. If a stranger walked in on their conversation, he'd never guess that both men were depending on each other for ballast in a stormy sea.

Five years ago Grobinski had been a shoo-in for a judicial seat in the state supreme court, but he had withdrawn before the election when he got the news about his daughter. On her way home from college she had been killed in a car accident. Two months later his wife, Mo, was diagnosed with cancer. After a painful five-year battle to combat it, Mo had finally licked the disease. And here was Dub, coat off, shirtsleeves rolled up, feet propped on the big oak conference table, stubbing out his cigar and slipping the ashtray behind an old copy of Black's Law Dictionary on the library shelf. He had found peace with himself and with the rest of the world. That was what Adam admired most about him. Maybe envied was more like it. Dub Grobinski, like his younger partner, had been through hell. But, unlike Adam, Dub had somehow found his way back.

As if he could read the other's mind, Dub asked, "How's Jilly?"

Adam clasped his hands together on the table, hiding the tremors that only he could see and feel. "Do you realize you ask me that every day?"

"That's because you never give me a satisfactory answer."

Adam resisted the desire to fold his arms across his chest like a shield. From Grobinski, he had learned the art of body language—an essential in the courtroom. He had that down pat. But his voice—that he had not yet mastered. It proved a traitor every time.

"She's okay."

"Yeah, that's what you always say."

"What the hell do you want me to say, Dub? She's—she's here. What more does everybody want from us?"

"It's not what *we* want, Adam. It's what you want that we're concerned about. It's what Jilly wants."

Envy. Yeah, that's what it was. Even while entering the forest of dark and twisting pain, Dub had somehow known how to mark the trail back to sanity. He had left behind crumbs of life to lead him back.

Adam hadn't done that. And what was more, most of the time he didn't even give a damn that he was lost.

"Why concern yourself? You can't help anyway. We want our life back. Can you do that for us?"

Dub shook his head. "Sorry, pal. That I can't do. You've got a new one now, and you two had better start living it."

Adam's bitterness, at times, was like a sinkhole. He could feel himself slipping into the ooze of despair and there was nothing, no branch, no hand, nothing to grab on to. "You're going to tell Jilly that, huh? Are you going to say, 'Hey, Jilly-girl, go on out there and live that great life that's ahead of you'?"

Dub leaned back in the chair, rocking it gently to and fro. "Have you bought her a tree yet?"

Adam glared at his partner. "We don't need any Christmas reminders, thank you very much."

"You may not, but what about Jilly?" He pulled his feet from the table and sat up in the chair. "Hey, I've got an idea. Why don't you bring her over to the house. You know how Mo is. She'll put on a big to-do. Christmas carols, fudge. She and Jilly can make some cookies together, the whole bit. She could invite some of her little buddies from school. Mo would love it. What do you say?"

"No."

"Just think about it."

"No."

The older man sighed. "You can't hide her away from the world, Adam."

"I know what's best for her."

A look of infinite sadness came across Dub's face in a flash and then, just as suddenly, disappeared. "It's been a year, my friend." He studied the troubled man across the table. "We're a world of walking wounded, Adam. But, you know, there's a certain strength that comes from accepting that."

Adam smirked. "Misery loves company, is that it?"

Dub shook his head. "I was thinking more that friends can sometimes help."

Adam sighed and looked away, wishing he could take back the things he often said and did, wishing he could say he was sorry. But he had buried himself in too many mistakes and sorries over the past year.

"It's Christmas, Adam. Time for renewal. Please think about bringing Jilly over. Just think about it."

"I'll think about it, Dub." But when Adam looked back at his colleague, all Dub saw was a man who had lost the ability to think. In law, he was as brilliant as ever. But his personal life was almost extinct. There seemed to be no life left in Adam Bech. What Adam needed, Dub knew, was a woman to soften the edges of his world. The right woman could work miracles.

As soon as Dub was gone for the day, Adam scribbled a note and dropped it onto his secretary's desk. When she came to work the next morning, she would read "Cancel dinner engagement Thursday night with Erica Manning. Whatever excuse you find appropriate."

## Chapter Two

Etta, the Welsh housekeeper who had been with the Bech family since the day Jilly was born, sat at the kitchen table, waiting out the storm that raged in front of her. Adam's hand slammed down on the table, and Etta's late afternoon cup of tea teetered on the delicate china saucer.

"I can't believe you let her go!" he yelled. "I can't believe you actually did it!"

Upstairs a door closed quietly.

"The Soames invited her, Mr. B. And Jilly said she wanted to go."

He sneered. "Oh, I'll just bet she did. What did you tell her? That she'd make all sorts of friends there? Or did you bribe her with Christmas cookies and milk?"

"I did no such thing, sir. You know I wouldn't have done such as that."

Tired beyond measure, Adam rested both hands on the table and leaned his weight into them. The fury wouldn't leave his body. It stayed clammed up inside, with nowhere to go. His face was creased with stubborn lines, but no more so than the housekeeper's. "Then why—why the hell did you let her go?"

Etta took a careful sip of tea and set down her cup. "You know how I feel about the way you protect her so."

"It's not your position to feel anything about the things I do. You are paid to watch her while I'm at work. Watch. Not send her off to parties."

"It's the Christmastime, sir."

"Not in this house."

She bent her head and murmured softly, "The God-child's birthday."

"Not in this house," he repeated through clenched teeth.

"Mrs. Bech wouldn't have liked it, sir, if I might say so."

Adam straightened up and walked over to the sink. He gripped the edge of the counter and stared through the window at the backyard. They had bought this large shady lot with the house on it when they were first married. Financially they had bitten off more than they could chew, but they were young and optimistic and had somehow managed to stay afloat until Adam made partner. Since then, money had never been an issue. It was the other things, peripheral things that went along with the rise in status, that had finally become issues between them.

He stared at the small vegetable patch, covered with a layer of grass clippings. The clay pots on the deck sat where they had sat for years, only now instead of being filled with a colorful profusion of winter pansies and chrysanthemums, they housed only dry stems and wayward blades of Johnsongrass.

Still facing the window, he said, "Mrs. Bech isn't here anymore."

Behind him at the table, Etta fiddled with her cup and saucer. Her employer was dealing with powerful demons, that she knew. And she didn't want or mean to add to his pain. But she had been raised on plain talk and honest words. She could speak nothing else. "I know the missus isn't here, sir. But you've got to carry on. And our little Jilly needs a jolly Christmas and to be with ones her own age. She needs chums. Playmates."

He swung around slowly, disoriented to the room and the conversation. His forehead creased with tension. "Chums? Playmates?" His smirk made cruel mockery of his pain. "You mean like the one at the park last week, that kid who suggested that they play hide-and-seek from the monster, from Jilly."

Etta had practically raised Jilly since she was a baby, and she loved her like a grandchild. But, for the moment, her own sorrow had to be placed aside. She looked up at her employer, at the man who, only a year before, had been so handsome in the evenings when he'd come home and whisk his beautiful little girl into his arms and wrap a loving arm around his pretty wife's shoulder. She wasn't sure she knew this man standing before her, this man with eyes the color and impenetrability of gun metal. He bore little resemblance to the Adam Bech she had grown accustomed to.

"She must learn to deal with it, Mr. Bech."

Adam reached out for the counter to steady himself. "Learn to deal with it? Learn what, pray tell? That the world's a hellhole to live in? That people are basically cruel and insensitive and that, by God, you'd better learn to live with it?" He glared at the housekeeper. "Huh?"

Etta refused to be intimidated. She was needed in the household, whether father and daughter realized it or not. She would not be pushed away by tragedy. "You don't believe that, Mr. B."

Adam turned those cold gray eyes on her and said in a voice that was thick with toxins, "From now on you will confine yourself to the duties of a housekeeper, Etta. You will clean and cook and shop for us. And then you will go home. You will not ever again—I repeat, ever again—take it upon yourself to decide what is best for my child. Do I make myself clear to you?"

Etta picked up the saucer, wrapping her hand around the cup of cold tea remnants. She carried them to the sink, where she rinsed them both and set them in the dishwasher. She reached for her large purse on the coatrack, then looked directly at her employer.

"As clear as a chime, Mr. Bech." She gave him no chance to chide her for insubordination. "Now, if you don't mind, I will be going up to Jilly's room to say good-day. She doesn't like it when I leave without saying a proper goodbye to her. I've left you a nice stew simmering there on the stove."

Rooted to a spot halfway between the counter and the table, Adam listened to the clip-clop of Etta's heavy black shoes as she strode purposefully through the dining room and into the front hall. Her feet carried her up the stairs toward Jilly's closed door.

Adam took an involuntary step backward and leaned against the counter. His eyes were squeezed shut. The kitchen, he realized, smelled of the stew and a cleaning agent that Etta had used on the counters and the floor. A pine smell. Marilyn obviously had liked the smell, so Etta had always used one of the pine products in her cleaning. Or was it the other way around? Maybe it was Etta who had decided that pine cleaners were the way to go. He just didn't know. He realized now how little interest he had taken in the everyday things. He hadn't been involved in the day-to-day household arrangements. Marilyn had taken care of all that.

With eyes closed and forehead creased, he mentally picked up another piece of his life's puzzle and examined it. Hadn't she, Marilyn, been the one to spend hours in the vegetable garden, the one who kept it free of weeds and bugs? Hadn't she been the one to fill every corner of the yard with colorful flowers and every corner of the house with antiques?

He pressed his fingertips against his temple and tried to remember if she had liked the smell of pine or not.

The door to Jilly's room closed, and he heard Etta clomp back down the stairs. The front door opened. Today was Friday, so she wouldn't be back until Monday. Until then, it would be all up to him. He had brought home a briefcase full of work to keep him busy over the weekend. And, of course, in the morning he would take Jilly down the street to the park. Early. Before all the other kids came out to play. Other than that, he figured they could maybe order a pizza tomorrow night. He would rent a movie for the VCR. They wouldn't have to go anywhere.

He had made a point of learning all the places around that delivered. Grocery stores, video stores, hamburger joints, pizza parlors, Chinese takeout. He kept a list on the refrigerator door where he didn't have to hunt for it. Sunday night they could order hamburgers. But Jilly loved Chinese the best, so maybe...

Shoving himself away from the counter, Adam rushed through the dining room and entry hall, flung open the front door, took the steps two at a time and bolted down the sidewalk like a man on fire. He caught up with Etta just as she was turning the corner onto Lancaster where she waited each afternoon for the bus.

"Etta!" he cried, running up to her, gasping for breath. He grabbed her by the shoulders and said, "Whose idea was it to use pine cleaners?"

Etta's eyes were wide with concern, not so much for herself as for her employer. From years of habit with Jilly, she now searched the father's face for any outward clues that could tell her if he was coming down with something. Maybe one of those twenty-four-hour things. "What are you talking about, Mr. B?"

"The pine cleanser that you use in the kitchen and in the bathrooms. Whose idea was it to use that?"

"Well, I don't know. Mine, I guess. I've been using Pine Sol ever since I can remember."

"Mrs. Bech didn't ask you to use it? It wasn't a scent she particularly liked?"

Etta pursed her lips and wondered exactly what it was that the man was driving at. "I don't think so. In fact, it took her a bit to get used to it, if I 'member it right. Why you askin', sir?"

"And the vegetables," he said. "Who planted them? Who picked them and put them in all those jars on the pantry shelf?"

Etta checked to see if the bus coming was hers. It wasn't, so she turned back to Adam. "The gardener planted them. I picked and canned them. But, Mr. B., I can hardly see why it is you're letting yourself fret about it so. We didn't plant anything this summer because we still have so much canned from last year. And—well, you hadn't requested us to do so. But if you would like . . ."

He stood there for a second, staring at her, wondering if he was losing his mind. It seemed that way sometimes. Now was one of those times.

"No. No, Etta," he said carefully, trying to hide his own bewilderment. His hands dropped from her shoulders and he backed up a few steps. "I—I was just wondering, that's all."

Etta tucked her chin in and watched with worried eyes as her employer turned and walked slowly— reluctantly, it seemed to her—back to the big brick house on Willow Lane.

ERICA DROVE FAST, her German-made car slicing easily around and between cars on the freeway. It was a Saturday, but that didn't mean it was a day off for Erica. Taking a day off meant lagging behind. There was too much to do. Too much to accomplish. She was always reaching for one goal after another. Finish one competition and there was always another looming on the near horizon. There was no time to slow down, to ease through a moment. If you did, her father had so often insisted, someone might usurp that moment from you.

If she could just wrap up this competition for *Focal Point*, then she could stop and relax a bit. But no, she knew that wouldn't end it. There would always be another one. Another competition. Her life was a series of them. She would never stop. If she let up, she would lose the momentum. It would mean second best. It would mean disappointing her father again. It would mean losing.

She tried to convince herself that it was her father's inevitable disappointment that made her drive by Adam Bech's house on this Saturday morning. She tried to tell herself that she wasn't disappointed that he'd broken their dinner date. But she knew it was a lie.

She was also irritated that he hadn't even bothered to cancel it himself. His secretary had done it for him. And not only that, but on Friday Erica had tried repeatedly to reach him by phone and was told each time that he was out. Simply out.

The truth was he was avoiding her. And she was bound and determined to find out why. She couldn't remember the last time someone had stood her up. And then to out and out avoid her!

She took the next exit off the freeway and wound down through the narrow tree-lined streets of Formosa. Zoned in the fifties for upper-crust living, it was like an untouched paradise of sweeping lawns, huge two-story homes and winding lanes that made it next to impossible for through traffic. Set like an island amidst the glaring steel-and-glass city, it beckoned to Erica on this warm Saturday morning in December.

She found the address easily enough: 4213 Willow Lane. The homes that graced the street were large and set back behind sweeping front lawns. Adam Bech's house was a white brick colonial with forest-green shutters on the windows. Quietly elegant, like the man himself.

Erica pulled into the curb and turned off the motor. By the reputation of the law firm and the size and style of his office, she had known the man was successful. But this house was simply magnificent.

Scattered leaves littered the sidewalk and curb, a reminder that here, in this city, fall and winter had no definable boundary, each overlapping onto the other, leaving a foot-dragging, undisciplined sense of nature. It was a crispness to the days that was lacking, and Erica longed for it desperately. She sat in her car with the sunroof open and watched a barefoot teenager in cutoff jeans and tank top, teetering precariously on a ladder as he strung lights along the nails pounded into his parents' eaves next door to Adam Bech's house. The mother came out, calling out a helpful suggestion to the boy, then went back into the house and closed the door. The suggestion had no visible effect on the boy. He moved the ladder over, climbed back up and strung the next four or five bulbs.

Erica got out of the car and walked up the long azalea-lined walkway to the front door. She rang the bell. After several tries, she realized he was not going to answer it. The house seemed almost deathly quiet, as if no one had lived there for a long time.

She walked back to the car and started the engine. Now what, she wondered. She had fully expected to find him home early on a Saturday morning.

She drove down the street slowly, watching the energetic joggers who had the fortitude to get up so early in the morning and circle the small lake on the right side of the road.

At the next stop sign, she paused, her gaze focused on two people who were walking down the sidewalk toward the small park at the end of the street. Her heart began to beat erratically. Even from behind and from half a block away, she felt sure that the man walking down the sidewalk was Adam Bech. Although why the realization that it was him should bring such a rapid acceleration to her pulse rate, she couldn't for the life of her understand. Yes, he was handsome, but she had been around plenty of handsome men before.

Her eyes moved from the man to the small figure walking beside him. A child—it hadn't occurred to her that he might have a family. Perhaps he had a wife at home, also. That would certainly explain why he had canceled their dinner engagement.

She moved the car forward slowly, staying well behind them. The contrast between the two was startling. His hair was dark, the little girl at his side was a bright blonde.

A little girl ... she had wondered occasionally what it would be like to have a little girl of her own. There was a vague need somewhere deep inside of her that surfaced now and then. It was the need to nurture. But then memories of her own childhood would always surface, and the need to nurture another was always washed away by the need to prove herself worthy in her father's eyes.

She watched Adam Bech and his daughter, spellbound by the way they walked, noticing that they seemed together but not together, isolated in some way from each other.

Like mismatched shadows that were thinly connected, they split apart as soon as they reached the park, the little girl veering off toward the swings at the far end, Adam settling himself with a magazine on a bench.

Erica pulled the car into the curb and sat with the engine idling. He looked so handsome sitting there in the early morning light. But he appeared so alone. He gazed off in the direction of the little girl, squinted against the sun and then lowered his eyes back to the magazine.

Erica switched off the engine and glanced into the rearview mirror, checking her makeup. She took a tissue and dabbed at the corner of her mouth. She glanced down at her suede skirt, brushing away an invisible speck of lint.

Before she completely lost her nerve, she opened the door and stepped out into a winter day that felt like Indian summer.

Adam watched Jilly ride high in the swing. He knew, in a few minutes, she would call out to him to push her. She always pleaded with him to go faster and higher. *Faster, Daddy, faster.* Did she not see the limitations? Was he the only one with any sense of reality? Jilly always thought she could do the same things as other kids. Etta took her to parties. Dub urged her to bake Christmas cookies. None of them seemed to get it.

He tried to focus on his magazine, but he glanced up when he realized someone was walking toward him. Usually no one showed up at the park until nine or ten on a Saturday morning. He was always gone long before then. His eyes narrowed as the figure moved closer, and his palms grew sweaty as recognition set in.

He saw her in parts, for the whole was too much to absorb at once. She glided rather than walked, a fluid line of motion, a shimmer of gold that reflected the morning sun, a swish of skirt, a pale ankle.

The panic multiplied when he felt the unwanted physical response. It came to him unbidden, like an invading foreigner.

"You canceled our dinner," she said, her voice soft but her mouth held tight. "Or I should say, your secretary canceled our dinner."

"I had to take some depositions."

"Your secretary said you had a court appointment."

"Right," he said, clearing his throat. "That was it." He felt a prisoner to the way she looked this morning, captured by the light in her hair and the cool blue of her eyes. He didn't know when he had ever met a more beautiful woman.

He glanced over at Jilly, but she was oblivious of the two adults. She was whizzing down the slide, then running back to the ladder to do it all over again. He hoped she'd stay over there. Out of harm's way.

"You are still going to do the show, aren't you, Mr. Bech?"

"I said I would," he answered, his voice laying distance between them.

Erica let out a slow breath, calming the waters that churned inside of her. Walking over here, she had convinced herself that this was strictly business, but one look at Adam Bech, sitting with his back against the morning sun, his gray eyes shadowed by the autumnlike haze, and she knew that she had lied to herself.

"The first segment of taping is set for Tuesday morning. Will that be a problem?"

He shook his head. "I don't think so."

She tried to smile. "No court appointments? No...depositions?"

He had the grace to look sheepish. "I shouldn't have had my secretary call you. I apologize for that, okay?"

She sat down beside him. "All is forgiven. But we really do need to go over some of this information."

He glanced across the park.

"Is that your daughter over there?"

He hesitated a beat too long. "Yes."

Erica squinted her eyes to focus on the child playing in the bright light. "She looks like she's having a good time."

Like that of a knife, the sharp emotional pain sliced through him, but he clenched his teeth until it went away. Still, he couldn't find an appropriate response for the woman beside him.

"Are you married, Mr. Bech?"

He turned around to face Erica. She was so beautiful. It would be very easy right now to reach out and touch her face or slide his fingers up the soft silk of her blouse. It had been so long now since he'd had these kinds of feelings, he wasn't sure he could trust himself with them now. "I was married. My wife died."

"I see." She didn't know what to say to him. She didn't know whether to feel relief or apprehension. She was glad he didn't have a wife; she would have been very disappointed to know there was no chance of ever getting to know Adam Bech on a more personal level. At the same time, she felt unequipped to deal with a man who had lost a wife—and probably a much-loved wife at that.

"What kind of information do we need to discuss?" He broke into her thoughts.

She took a deep breath, relieved that they were going to move onto more stable ground. "I'd like to know why you chose to defend Mr. and Mrs. Tobias."

"Everyone is entitled to the best defense possible."

"Please, Mr. Bech, don't pull that on me in the interview. You see, I—and the viewers—want something other than pat answers. We want something new and fresh and tantalizing. Something that might provoke the audience and stoke a fire in them. Not stock footage."

*Tantalizing?* She didn't know that he was too tired to tantalize and his own fires had long ago turned to ash. Of course, he reasoned, the world didn't have to know that. Not if he didn't let them see it. He had learned over the past year to play the games that society expected. Even from where he sat on the sidelines, he could play them, and no one ever knew the truth.

"As I said, Miss Manning, everyone—"

"Please call me Erica. On the show, I'll expect you to call me by my first name, so we might as well start now."

"All right."

"Now—what were you saying?"

He couldn't think. He couldn't seem to remember anything. He glanced over, remembering that somewhere on the playground was a little girl who belonged to him. There she was, swinging again. Her favorite. He wondered what she was thinking right now as she swung back and forth. He didn't have to wonder what Erica Manning would think when she saw Jilly. He knew.

He checked his watch. "I need to get home." It would be risky to stay longer. Any minute now, Jilly was going to call for him to come push her in the swing or on the merry-go-round, and he certainly didn't want his daughter to be confronted with someone like Erica. "I have to take my daughter home, so, uh . . ."

Erica frowned. Two minutes ago he didn't seem in any hurry. Now, all of sudden, there was this big rush. What was his problem? "Maybe we could talk at your house."

"No," he answered too quickly, then made the mistake of looking at Erica's bewildered face. Once again, he was snared by physical longings that he couldn't control, and the words seemed to spill from his mouth of their own accord. "Would you like to have dinner tonight?"

"I—well, yes, I would, but—"

"What's your address? I'll pick you up at seven-thirty."

"I have a town house not too far from here." She tore off a piece of paper from her notepad and wrote her address and phone number. She handed it to him with a confused smile. "Am I going to get a call from your secretary at about six-thirty?"

"No," he said quietly, glancing over at Jilly. She was starting to walk toward them, so he stood up and, with his hand resting lightly against Erica's lower back, he ushered her toward her car. "We'll go over the case. I promise. Tonight."

Completely baffled by the man's unpredictability but secretly thrilled at the chance of dinner with him, she let him lead her to the car. Before she could start the engine and pull away from the curb, Adam had walked over to his daughter and was pushing her high on the swing. With the windows rolled down, Erica could hear the childish squeals of delight, and she wondered once again what it would be like to have a child of her own.

# Chapter Three

"Wow," Adam breathed softly, but loud enough for her to hear.

Erica stepped into the hall and closed the door behind her, making sure it was locked. "Wow, yourself."

He glanced down at his clothes. "It's just a suit, like all the others in my closet. Not a lot of variety in men's fashion."

Erica smiled up at him. "This is just a dress."

His eyes had grazed down the backless black dress when she'd turned to lock the door. "Hardly."

She listened to the tone in his voice, pleased at the mixture of boyish awe and middle-aged respect.

He took her to one of the finest restaurants in the city. A magnificent white Christmas tree stood in the middle of the dining room, reaching almost two stories high. The large glass windows that circled the room reflected the glow from the tree's thousands of tiny white lights. A pianist was playing a stylized version of "Carol of the Bells" as they were seated near the windows.

"This is beautiful. I've never been here before at Christmas time."

The sadness that always hit in unsuspecting moments struck Adam now full force. He looked at the tree and the reflected lights and suddenly wished he hadn't come. "It's nice," he answered, thinking only of how much simpler it would have been had he stayed home tonight. He didn't understand the complex thoughts that kept swirling through his head. It bothered him that he found this woman so appealing. He shouldn't have left Jilly with Dub and Mo. He should have stayed home with her. It was wrong for him to be out like this with a beautiful woman when his wife and his little girl . . .

"Hello," she said, waving her hand in front of him. She smiled and cleared her throat, indicating the waiter who hovered over them, poised to take the drink order. And, while knowing that he shouldn't be here and filled with guilt over the selfishness of it all, he added to the idiocy by ordering a bottle of Moët et Chandon.

When the waiter was gone, Erica regarded him closely. "I thought I'd lost you there for a minute."

No, unfortunately, he was here. On a date. With a beautiful woman. He was just going to have to make the best of it. Later he would make it up to Jilly. "No, I'm here."

"I'm glad."

He stared at the soft curve of her red lips, barely resisting the urge to reach over and trace the line of it with his finger. "I am, too," he said, knowing he meant it, hating the fact that he did—but not hating it enough. He was glad to be here with her. She made him feel like a man again. He couldn't help but notice the stares they received when they walked in. Heads turned to look at her first and then at him. All guilt aside, it made him proud to have her walking in beside him.

The champagne came and, with a to-a-successful-interview toast, they began to relax and enjoy each other's company. Adam seemed more comfortable when the conversation was centered on her rather than on him, and he kept her talking about her past as much as possible.

After they ordered dinner, Erica told him about the beauty pageants and the continuous stream of contests. "It seems like I was always away from home at this time of year. I really longed for a Christmas like my friends had. But Dad—well, he didn't see it that way."

Adam leaned back when the lobster bisque was set before him. "What about your mother? Where was she?"

Erica shivered from a sudden chill and turned her gaze toward the reflected lights of the window. "My mother was not healthy. She had rheumatoid arthritis and spent a great deal of time in clinics. She died when I was fourteen."

"I'm sorry."

Erica looked at Adam. His expression of sympathy was genuine and she knew that, with this man, nothing short of honesty would ever do. "I'm sorry, too. I never really knew her very well. My father—hmm, let's just say he was not the in-sickness-and-in-health type. He hired lots of help." She stared at her full plate. "I think sometimes that I should have done something like that."

"Like what?"

"Like taken care of her myself." She shook her head to dispel the somber mood. "Anyway, I like

Christmas even though I've never had the typical one.
I sort of envy you, having a child to share it with. That
must be nice."

Adam took a sip of champagne. *No one has to see
the pain if you don't let it show.* That was the trick.
*Keep it hidden from the world.* "Yeah, it's great."

They ate lobster bisque, redfish, and topped it off
with Bananas Foster. During dinner, she asked him
about his law career and about some of his more interesting cases. Finally she got the nerve to ask him
about his wife.

"It was a year ago," he said. "December 5. We were
out in the Gulf on our boat. We had a group of friends
with us. Another boat rammed us.... It's not something I really like to talk about."

"Okay. I won't ask anymore."

"Maybe we should discuss the interview."

Erica stared across the table at this fascinating,
complex man. There was so much inside him that she
wanted to see, and yet there was so little that he was
willing to reveal. There were brief moments when she
knew that he was attracted to her. She could tell by the
way his eyes shone when he looked at her. She could
see it in the upward tilt of his mouth. And she found
herself wanting to reach across the table to touch the
strong fingers that encircled his champagne glass.

She kept her hands on her side of the table and took
a deep breath. "You were starting to tell me this
morning why you defended the Tobiases. I think it's
an important point and one the audience is going to
have some difficulty understanding."

"Why is it so difficult to understand?"

Erica shrugged. "A young man is accused of the
brutal murder of a high school girl. She was an honor

student. A cheerleader. People can relate to someone like her. She was all-American, you know."

"You mean the public was ready to convict the boy on the basis of who the victim was, rather than on the facts of the case."

She shrugged. "I don't know. Maybe. But the fact that the boy's parents had information that would have been useful to the state's investigation and yet refused to give that information on religious grounds—I don't know, I think it's very difficult to understand, Adam. Did you make a judgment call here, or was this just a case of a client with money walking into your office?"

He cringed slightly. "You don't beat around the bush, do you?"

"To be successful in a show like this, you sometimes have to go for the jugular. I hope you won't take offense."

He grinned. "I think I can handle it."

She smiled back. "I'm sure you can."

He paused for a minute, trying to focus on the topic at hand, but it was difficult when she smiled at him that way. It made him feel hot and liquefied inside. It made him want things he couldn't even define.

"I chose to defend Ben Tobias and his wife because I believe firmly that parents have the right—no, more like the obligation—to protect their children in any way humanly possible."

"But a crime was committed, Adam. That has to make a difference."

He shook his head.

"Oh, come on," she argued. "You can't possibly believe that—that harboring a criminal comes under those protective rights." Watching him as she spoke, she studied those gray eyes of his posing as two shields assigned to protect and defend. The rest of his features were lean and spare, and his dark hair was disciplined into place, but it was the eyes that held her riveted, making her want to penetrate the barrier.

Adam leaned forward, resting his elbows on the table, his hands clasped beneath his chin. "Erica, to say the Tobiases were harboring a criminal is to place judgment."

"How can you *not* say that?"

"Look, Daniel Tobias was arrested. He was arraigned, bail was set, a trial took place before a jury of twelve, and he was acquitted. That's the procedure in this country."

"But his parents had vital information that could have changed the outcome of that trial."

He cocked his head and smiled at her. "What information was that?"

Her lips tightened and she tried to find it in her to be mad at him for the patronizing look and tone. "Are you going to do this to me during taping?"

"What's that?"

"Look at me that way."

"What way?"

Her mouth twisted sideways. "I think you know. Yes, I think you know exactly what you're doing."

He shrugged innocently and sat back in the chair.

She too sat back, looking out over the restaurant, thinking about how often her father had patronized her or prodded and goaded her. And if she ever complained, she was rewarded with a wounded and innocent look that only someone guilty as hell could produce.

"Where do the rights of parents end, Adam?" She turned back to him. "How much control should they be allowed over their children's lives?"

She saw the shift in his expression. It was just a flicker that registered an awareness of altered ground, as if she had stepped too close. She could hear the tinkling of silverware and the murmured conversations from nearby tables in the pause while he looked at her. Just looked at her and said nothing. In those brief moments, she felt her heart hammer against her rib cage.

Finally he said in a slow, quiet voice, "I'm not sure there is a limit."

He saw that she was frowning at him, just slightly, more confused than anything else. But what could he do to set her straight? What could he say to make her understand how it was?

"I can't agree with that."

He tried to smile. "No, I suppose not."

"I'll be asking you things like this, Adam. On the program."

He kept the panic tightly reined, but she saw it anyway. And he knew that she saw it. "It's your show."

The lights on the Christmas tree brightened and she felt pressure behind her eyes. It had to be the lights. She never cried in public. And she never succumbed to it in private unless there was a very good reason. She looked at Adam Bech and knew that there was no reason for her to cry, and yet—right now that was exactly what she wanted to do. "Thank you for the dinner, Adam. I think I'd like to go home now."

He quietly asked for the check, drove her straight to her town house and walked her to the door. It was only at the last moment that she saw him waver. Just for a split second did she see the question in his eyes, the temptation to ask if he could come in with her.

Had he asked, she knew exactly what she would have said.

"LAST YEAR, on the morning of March 2, a heinous crime was committed..."

Under the hot lights, Adam was sweating. But Erica, it seemed, was in her element. Not a drop of perspiration dared appear on the surface of her flawless face. The makeup artists had made sure of it. Her eyes never failed to beguile him and, although he once again thought she looked like an angel, he knew the minute the questions began, that she was anything but.

He listened as she dispassionately stated the facts of the crime. Her voice remained professionally dry, a practiced noncommittal, but her eyes had become like two impudent blue sparks in a contained fire. Alive, glowing. Under the lights, before the cameras, she was in her element. On the surface, she was cool and collected, but beneath the outer layer of composure, she was most definitely on fire. He watched with fascination as the transformation took place. It reminded him somewhat of his own early days in the courtroom, and he decided that perhaps he and Erica Manning were not so different from each other.

"This morning's guest, Adam Bech, is the attorney who chose to defend Mr. and Mrs. Benjamin Tobias."

The way she said it sounded to Adam less like an introduction and more like an indictment. He felt another drop of sweat roll down his neck, but he didn't dare wipe it away. Not on television.

Erica swiveled in her upholstered chair and faced him. In the periphery, she knew the roving cameras were trained on her every movement. She took in a shallow breath, hoping the air would cleanse her of this displaced sensation. She hadn't seen him since Saturday night, but she had found it extremely difficult to think of anyone or anything but him since. No man had ever affected her that way.

She wanted to get to know him, and yet she was afraid of things she might learn. His looks and his voice were magnetic, and yet there was a sadness in him that had formed a solid barrier. She didn't know how to get through it. She didn't even know if she wanted to. She wasn't used to commitments to other people. She didn't know how to fulfill anyone else's needs. And yet, she found herself attracted to a man who had lost his wife, a man who had needs she couldn't even begin to comprehend. No, simplicity in her life was what she needed, not someone like Adam Bech.

Trying to remain as detached as possible, she outlined the highlights of the trial for her audience, then turned to Adam. "The parents of Daniel Tobias had vital information that could have changed the outcome of that trial."

"What information was that, Erica?" His eyes locked with hers and she saw the baiting glint, the teasing smile that made it clear he remembered them going over this information the other night. She had said she would ask him these things on the set. Well, he would answer them just as he had before.

Erica tried to keep the glare out of her look. He was baiting her and she didn't like it one little bit. She had to keep her edge, remain cool and objective. Thinking of the audience who would watch the program, she could see them out there changing the channel or throwing an old sock at the television screen. She thought of her producer wincing in the control booth. She thought of her father's face with its rigid jaw and sharp lines of disapproval.

She turned her winning smile to the camera. "We could sit here all day and argue about what that information was, *Mr.* Bech. The papers have been speculating about it for months. But the issue at stake is whether the Tobiases had the right to withhold any information that could be used in investigating this murder. It *was* murder."

"That fact has been established," he said. "But that was not my case. The case I was involved in was the *State versus Benjamin Tobias.*"

"And were you personally involved?" she asked.

He frowned. "I'm not certain I understand the question."

"Wasn't there any feeling, one way or another, that maybe your defense was turning the murder of a young girl into a travesty? Didn't you ever feel that justice was not being served?"

"Justice for whom?"

Erica sat up straighter and tilted her chin out, knowing that her voice must have a tremendous impact on the home audience. "For Annie Boulton, Mr. Bech. Annie Boulton, the sixteen-year-old girl who was brutally murdered on March 2."

Adam hesitated perhaps a beat too long. But her voice, so soft and earnest, had caught him by surprise. And she had wedged him into a corner where he was put on the defensive. She was good at this, there was no doubt about it. But so was he. And he wasn't going to let her seductive voice and eyes lure him away from the facts. "I told you, our firm had nothing to do with the Boulton trial. The only connection between the two cases is, in my opinion, a peripheral one, and—"

"A peripheral one! You must be joking, Mr. Bech. How can you believe that?"

Damn, but she was stimulating! He felt the heat in his body intensify, and he knew it had nothing to do with lights and nerves. It had to do with her and what he wished he was doing with her right now instead of this. But, seductive or not, he wasn't about to let her get the best of him.

He smiled indulgently. "You, like many others in the community, are under the impression that crime and justice can be explained on a linear graph. They cannot," he said. "It is like a mosaic, each piece separate from all the others, but adding to the whole."

At his smile, Erica felt her blood boil. There it was again, that magnetic smile of his that both seduced and patronized at the same time. Oh, he was infuriating! The things she would say to him right now if they were alone...

All her life men had patronized and indulged her. And, in truth, it had helped her to gain what she had today. But she was more than a precious poodle on a leash. And this man—and her audience—was going to know that.

"Mr. Bech," she said, simmering like an Irish stew, "you are evading the issue here. What we are talking about is the rights of parents. Do parents have the right to protect their children even if they are wrong?"

"But who is to say the Tobiases were wrong? Define *wrong* for me."

She had thought this would be such a simple interview. Bring Adam on, put him in the hot seat where he would squirm a bit before answering, and then she could go back to the office and watch the program ratings skyrocket.

The key to a successful program, her producer always insisted, was to make the guest relax and open up, but to never, never let him come out looking better than the host. So she had gone over the trial notes time and time again. She had gone on a date with the person she was interviewing, for God's sake! She thought she had a handle on this.

It should have been a winning combination. She had prepared and she had this terrific-looking man to prod. Audiences loved that kind of play between host and guest. But she had certainly not expected him to be so difficult—so set in his ways.

Nor had she expected to feel as if she were walking through a carnival fun house with the man. Everything was askew, tilted and out of proportion. One moment she wanted nothing more than to be alone with him and to feel his hands roam across her body. And the next moment all she wanted to do was to punch him.

There had to be a way to turn this around to her advantage. A way to get to him the way he was getting to her. She obviously couldn't compete with him over the facts of the case or the technicalities and subtle nuances of interpretive law. But she could hit the personal angle, taking into account the audience's emotions.

"Where do the rights of parents end, Mr. Bech?" she asked, going for the Achilles' heel, knowing it was the only way to regain the upper hand. "How much control should they be allowed over their children's lives?"

The clock above the stage door right ticked off a four-second pause as he stared at her, letting her know that he was aware of what she was doing. And he wasn't going to give her the satisfaction of making him squirm. He smiled, but only she could see that it didn't reach his eyes. "Some people would say there is no limit."

"Some people?" she repeated. "Like you, Mr. Bech?"

"I haven't really thought about it that much."

Her eyes narrowed and she pursed her lips, trying hard to hold in the retort that so badly wanted voice.

"Well, tell me this," she said. "You say that the Tobiases were protecting their son. Could it be that they were merely protecting themselves?"

Something tightened in Adam's chest, but he took a deep breath to ease the knot. She was talking about the case. The audience knew that. The stage crew knew that. *It's not personal,* he reminded himself. *This is separate, apart from the world you live in. Don't let them see the truth.* "I'm not sure I understand the question."

"You are a parent, isn't that correct, Mr. Bech?"

There was only the slightest hesitation in his voice, but his breath accelerated. "That's correct."

"A little girl, yes?"

His heart beat like a jackhammer inside his chest, his jaw grew tight. "That's right."

"So therefore you must believe that you have the ultimate right to protect your child from what you perceive—I repeat—what you perceive is harmful to her."

How much did she know? How much of his life had she penetrated? He couldn't believe that she would use it against him. Not this woman who took his breath away every time he was near her.

"Is that what you believe, Mr. Bech?"

"Without question."

This time, Erica saw that there was no hesitation. The answer had come forcefully and with conviction. A new potency had been added to the dialogue, to his voice, that she couldn't quite pinpoint. Was it anger? Fear? His eyes were like two hard marbles and, for a moment, she wondered if she had gone too far. Still, her career was at stake here. She had to regain the lead, and that's all there was to it.

"What if you are wrong?" she asked softly, effectively.

The knot tightened inside of him. He cleared his throat. "Wrong about what?"

"About this ultimate right to protect, to guard, to control the lives of children. What if the Tobiases were wrong, Mr. Bech?"

Adam stared at Erica sitting across from him, waiting with almost ferocious intent for his answer, her blue eyes drilling into him. He wished he'd never laid eyes on her. He wished he had never been foolish enough to ask her out.

"What if?" she repeated.

He finally spoke. "There are no 'what ifs,' Erica. There are only end results. Cause and effect. We make choices in life—one after another—and then we live with them. The Tobiases made theirs."

"I see," she said. "And some people live and some die. A young girl is murdered, a young boy goes free. Just choices, choices that we live with. Is that it, Mr. Bech?"

She was talking about the case. He knew that. The audience knew that. Still, his palms felt hot and wet. And his chest was filled with an ache that wouldn't go away. "That's right," he said.

"Well, I certainly hope, Mr. Bech, that you can live with yours."

In his eyes, she watched the impenetrable shield drop into place. "I guess I have to, don't I?"

Erica's eyes were glued on his face. Heat traveled through her, making her feel as if more than their gazes and words were locked in a duel. It was as if their bodies and minds were entwined in a painful struggle for dominance. Adam Bech was only sharing her lights and her cameras, but she felt drained. She felt as if they had torn something from each other, stripped away the protective shield and left each other bare and bleeding.

He had pulled something from her, yanked emotions and sensations that she didn't have to spare. It was partially physical, she felt sure. After all, he was a man who would rattle any woman's composure; she had felt that draw since the first moment she met him in his office. But there was more to it than that, more than just a physical yen. He had left her feeling reduced and exhausted.

She needed more time with him. She needed to feel the way she had before the show—on top of the world, successful, perfectly in sync. And she knew instinctively that he who had drained her would have to be the one to refill her. It was, without a doubt, the most debilitating sensation she had ever experienced in her life.

She glanced at the clock on the wall. There seemed to be much left unsaid. A box had been opened, but only the surface contents had been touched. Something provocative lay buried beneath. She didn't want this to end.

"I wish we had more time, Adam Bech. I feel that we have only just begun."

He regarded her closely, wondering if she was right about that. Hoping she was wrong. She was beautiful, but he had no room for beauty in his life. No room for passion. Not anymore.

Before he could crystallize his response, the bright lights faded, the stage fell into a series of shadows, and Erica unclipped her microphone.

Adam stood up and, without looking at her again, walked to the door and flung it open. The eyes of the stunned crew jumped from Adam to Erica and back again. She hurried past their curious stares to follow Adam into the hallway.

He was standing before the elevator, stabbing the button as if his finger were a knife. When he saw Erica coming toward him, he abandoned the elevator and headed for the back stairway. The door was closing behind him when she reached it.

"Adam, wait. Please."

He was halfway down the first flight of stairs and he stopped, his back toward her, his hand gripping the handrail.

She hurried down and stopped on the step beside him. "I didn't mean to upset you, Adam. It was the show. I told you I would ask you questions like that. I thought you understood. It was the show."

He was staring straight ahead, his chest rising and falling rapidly with each heavy breath. He wasn't going to look at her. He wouldn't do that to himself.

He slowly turned and his eyes locked greedily on her face. In one swift movement, he wrapped his hand behind her neck, pushed her up against the wall and pressed his body into hers. His mouth fastened hungrily over hers, tasting, probing, searching for clues to his own madness. What he was doing was insane and he knew it, but something kept him from retaining his mental grasp.

Her arms lifted, her hands locking behind his neck. This was what she had wanted him to do from the moment she'd met him. It was crazy. She didn't react this way to men. Especially a man who only moments before had acted as if he hated her.

He tore his mouth away and looked up at the ceiling, his breath falling quick and ragged between them.

"This is a mistake, Erica."

Her own breath was shallow and rapid as it mingled with his. "What is?"

"This whole thing. This isn't the way I want it."

She moved into him, pressing her lips against his throat, not wanting to let him go. "Come to my house, tonight, Adam. For dinner."

He let go of her and leaned onto his palms against the wall. Her mouth moved across his neck, her lips barely touching his sensitized skin. But his eyes remained closed. "Yes." He hesitated. "No."

She stopped kissing him and looked up at his face. "Why not?"

He pulled away and once again grasped the stair railing for support. "I can't. I have—" He looked at her. "I have a daughter, remember?"

How quickly she had forgotten, she realized. But then, she had never had to share anyone before. Her father had devoted his every moment to her. People had sacrificed to help Erica go where she wanted to go in life. She had never had to sacrifice anything. She had never dreamed of the time when she might have to share a man with a child. And yet she sensed that this one child held a special place in her father's life. To be with one would obviously mean she would have to be with the other.

"I'd like to meet her, Adam."

His eyes swept over Erica's flawless face and he chuckled without mirth. "I don't think so."

She frowned. "Why not?"

The fear for Jilly was always with him, never giving him a moment's rest, never letting him forget for even a second what he had done to her. "Take my word for it, it wouldn't work."

"I don't understand, Adam. I thought—I thought you and I were—were building something here."

He shook his head. "I'm not ready for this, Erica, okay?"

"Because of your wife?"

He was silent for so long she wondered if he'd understood the question. He had. He was just trying to decide if it was better for her to believe that than the truth. "Yes," he said. "Because of my wife."

As she watched him walk down the stairs, his final words rang over and over in her mind. But in some deep part of her, it refused to settle into truth. Whether it was wishful thinking or an unwillingness to accept the realities of life, she didn't know. All Erica did know was that she wasn't going to let him walk out of her life with a statement like that. He could not have kissed her the way he had if his wife had been any factor at all. That kiss said things about Adam Bech that Erica was not about to ignore.

# Chapter Four

Larry poked his head around the corner of Erica's nine-by-nine cubicle. "How's my girl? Come up with anything for the next program yet?"

Erica closed the file of news clippings she had been studying. "Not yet."

"Well," he said, fixing to go, "you'll come up with something."

"Wait, Larry. Can you come sit for a sec? I need to talk to you."

"It's Friday, babe. I don't want to hang around too long. Don't you have a date or something?"

She shook her head. "No."

"Well," he said, "I'm going to meet Stan and some of the guys over at Laddy's later. Why don't you join us?"

"Maybe."

He opened a folding chair and put it beside her desk. He sat down. "So what's up?"

An assistant came around the corner and, apologizing for the interruption, handed Erica another file. "Here's the stuff you wanted on Bech."

"Thanks, Molly."

"Bech?" asked Larry. "Isn't that old news?"

Erica pulled out a couple of the newspaper clippings she had been perusing when Larry walked in. "I don't know. I don't think so. I've been going over this Tobias case. It's a fascinating story, Larry, and I think the audience is going to want more on it. I don't think we should just let the thing drop."

"That was yesterday's news, Erica. You've done two tapings this week with Bech, the program ran yesterday. It was good. Lots of response. Now let's move on."

A sense of desperation clutched her. She didn't want to feel this way, but she couldn't get rid of it. For the past three days, since the intense taping on Tuesday and the chilly, shorter one on Wednesday, she had tried to push it away, tried to put it into some kind of perspective, but it wouldn't let go of her. It held her fast, leaving little room in her mind for other thoughts. But she had to be careful here. She certainly didn't want Larry to think this was some sort of obsession. Rationality and calm were what was called for.

"Don't you think that's one of the problems with the show, Larry? I mean we stay on the surface of lots of different subjects, but we don't delve into them enough."

"This isn't a delving program, Erica. Surface is what we are. That's what the marketing studies show the audience wants. If they wanted to delve into the inner workings of the judicial system, they'd tune into PBS. Or—" he grinned "—*People's Court*."

"But you said the response on the segment was good."

"It was great. Lots of phone calls."

"So—"

"So, Erica, those calls were more in reference to Adam Bech than to any legal or moral issue discussed. Lots of *women* callers, if you get my drift." Larry grinned.

Erica understood him—all too well. She chose to ignore his comment. "But the show is supposed to be about—"

Larry held up his hand. "Listen, babe, we can sit here all day and argue about what the show should be or shouldn't be. The bottom line is that we appeal—as you should know—primarily to women viewers. Those who called on the segment were much more interested in Bech than in the Tobias trial. Now—" he again held up his hand before she could argue "—I want you to have an idea for your next show on my desk Monday morning." He lowered his voice. "I don't think I need to remind you that you're the one on trial here."

Fatigue swept down over her, but she couldn't let it show. She had to stay up. Always on. Always the beaming, congenial beauty queen. "No, Larry," she said, hiding the weariness. "You don't have to remind me."

Deciding that he would anyway, he said, "I had to push to get you included in this lineup for *Focal Point*. You know that."

"Yes."

"The producer didn't want you," Larry added, blasting her with facts she already knew by heart. "He wanted to put you on *Women's World* at midday, where viewers could look at your gorgeous face and then go away feeling that the world's a real nifty place."

She picked up her pencil and began tapping it against the desk. "How trite."

"The world's a trite place, kiddo. You, of all people, should know that."

"How nice of you to point that out," she said, feeling worse than ever.

Larry scooted to the front of the chair and leaned his forearms on her desk. "Look, babe, my point is that you've got to work at this. Now, come on, don't let me down. What about that boating safety program you were going to do? Move ahead with that."

"Adam Bech's wife was killed in a boating accident."

"Yeah, so what's your point?"

She frowned at Larry. "I can't go from an interview with him and then jump right into a program that—well, that's like a personal assault on him."

"Personal assault? This has nothing to do with Adam Bech, Erica. This has to do with us. With you. With your job."

Why was she having so much trouble separating the two anymore? Why couldn't she keep her focus where it belonged? "What is Karen doing on her next show?"

"That chemical spill over near the bay. But don't you worry about her, Erica. Worry about what you're going to do."

"I have to worry about her, Larry!" she shouted, then shook her head in self-disgust and lowered her voice. "This show is important to me."

"And to me. But you're letting what they do psyche you out."

"I just want to come out ahead on this, okay?"

"Why?"

She stared at him as if he were daft. "Why? Why the hell do you think? I want the full-time host position."

His gaze narrowed on her face and he nodded slowly. "Right. You or your old man?"

"What is that supposed to mean?"

"I mean he's the one who puts all this pressure on you to win, win, win, isn't that right?"

Erica looked away and spoke softly. "Everyone expects me to win. They always have. I've always been the winner, Larry. That's the way life is meant to be played."

"Well, all I know is you'd better decide who you're living your life for—you or big daddy." He stood up. "Let's do the boating segment, Erica. I liked it from the beginning. Okay?"

No, it wasn't okay, but Erica didn't say that. Instead she said, "Larry, I know what everyone around here thinks of me. They don't think I belong here. They don't think I deserve this. They see me as—as cleavage and straight teeth. But I'm more than that, Larry. I want you to see that."

Larry turned and gave her a lascivious grin. "Babe," he said with a wink, "you do have nice teeth."

When he was gone, she stared at the thin fiberboard half wall that separated her office from the next one. Boating safety. How could she possibly expect to compete with Manda and Karen doing stories like that? Karen was going to do something on the chemical spill, something that affected the whole area. And after all, who really gave a flying fig if boating was safe or not? Especially in December. Especially at Christmas! St. Nick on a catamaran. Right.

With her elbows on the desk, Erica leaned into her hands. She was so tired she could hardly form a coherent thought.

She pulled the stack of papers over in front of her. There was something more to this Benjamin Tobias story and she was determined to find it, if not in the trial transcript, then in the lives of the Tobiases or maybe even in the background search on Adam Bech that Molly had brought her. She couldn't begin to admit to herself that the background search had nothing to do with the show and everything to do with her need to see Adam again at any cost.

She set aside the transcripts and opened the new file. There was a grainy black-and-white newspaper photograph of Adam. And in the stack of news articles, Molly had underlined any quotes by him. There was a two-page typewritten biographical sketch. Adam Sloan Bech, forty-two, had graduated summa cum laude from Rice University in 1969, graduated the University of Texas School of Law, joined the firm of Grobinski and Kettering in 1974 and became a partner five years later. The sketch listed the professional organizations to which he belonged, cited his home address and phone number and mentioned that he was a widower with one child, a daughter.

Erica flipped to the second page and read on. Her heart began to pound, and she felt prickles along the back of her neck. She found another news clipping on the bottom of the pile. She flinched when she caught the headline and then, with a growing sense of dread, read slowly through the entire article and went back and read it again.

Suddenly and with a force that sent her thoughts reeling backward, she saw clearly what Adam had been so careful to keep hidden—his daughter, his little girl, had been badly burned in the boating accident that had claimed his wife. But no, it couldn't be true. She had watched them walking down the sidewalk, a man and little girl, side by side, bound in some undefinable way. She picked up the grainy photograph. Just looking at this two-dimensional slice of Adam Bech was enough to send her senses spinning. Here was a man who had it all—looks, money, success, prestige in the community. He was perfect.

No, it couldn't be true about his daughter. And yet, it was. He had been holding a little girl's hand, crossing the street to the playground. The little girl had run off to the far side of the park. When she wanted to be pushed on the swings, she had come back toward her father, and Adam had practically shoved Erica into her car.

When she had mentioned that she'd like to meet his daughter, he had said it would never work.

He had said he wasn't ready for a relationship—because of his wife.

But it wasn't his wife, at all. It was his daughter.

A parent's right to protect his child—*there is no limit,* he had said.

Erica stared once again at the photograph of the man. *There are no what ifs,* he had said. *Only cause and effect. Only choices.*

She had entertained thoughts of him. She couldn't deny that. And there was something about him that was so intriguing, so compelling, that she had wanted any excuse to see him again. But now…now all that was changed.

In the far reaches of her mind, Erica could still hear her mother's painful moans echoing through the open spaces of their large house. She could hear her father's lament. *Don't ever, ever saddle yourself with some cripple the way I did.* She felt him reach out and touch her face. *If it weren't for you, Princess, my life wouldn't be worth living. I hope you realize that.*

Erica Manning lived in a full and pristine world, a world that left no room for sacrifice or disabilities or less than perfect accoutrements. Adam Bech had seemed the perfect accompaniment for her life. But, because of unforeseen circumstances, he now was burdened with an afflicted child.

God, how could this have happened! She had wanted so badly to get to know him, to feel his arms around her again, to feel his hot insistent mouth against hers once more. She had thought that he was perfect for her. But now—

She remembered her father once telling her that children, on the whole, were a burden. She was different, he had said, because she had been born perfect. Perfection or burden was the philosophy Erica had been handed. That didn't leave much room for anything in between.

So this was the way it was to be. She was to lose Adam Bech before she ever even had him. And to top it off, Larry wanted a story on boating safety. All she had to do was drag in the personal story of Adam Bech and his family. Larry would be elated. The show, with all the human drama and tragedy, would be a surefire winner. All she had to do was exploit one child. All she had to do was rub Adam Bech's face in his own misery. She could wipe Manda and Karen out of the competition for good.

She clenched her fists and squeezed her eyes shut. It wasn't fair. She shouldn't be in this position. Why did this have to happen to her!

She glanced up through her doorway and into the center of the open newsroom as the last person to leave unplugged the lights on the Christmas tree. Erica stared for a long time at the darkened tree. Disgust washed through her, but whether it was for the man whose life she had just invaded or for herself, she didn't know. Erica Manning didn't have a clue.

THE EVENING EDITION of the newspaper was spread out over Parker Manning's couch. He sat with a corner of it on his lap, his stockinged feet on the coffee table, while Erica curled her legs beneath her in the wingback chair across from the table. The coffee server and cups, black lacquer edged in gold, sat between them. On the walls of his well-appointed condominium were framed photographs and articles, all touting the beauty and achievements of his one and only daughter.

Erica rarely dated. When she was younger, her dad had never let her. He didn't want anyone or anything interfering with her primary focus, which was to compete in the pageants. And any boys who came to the house to call on her quickly lost interest when they realized that to date Erica Manning meant having to deal with her father. It just wasn't worth the trouble.

Men still tended to stay away, but for a different reason now. Because of her looks and because of all the contests she had won, they assumed that she had men lined up a block long to get a date with her. Not wanting to face the competition, they stayed a safe distance away.

Erica often spent quiet Friday nights having dinner with her father and then going home alone. She tried not to equate aloneness with loneliness, but sometimes it was hard not to. Especially tonight. Especially when Adam Bech lay so heavily on her mind and kept her thoughts in turmoil.

"You never said what you thought about the program yesterday."

Parker looked over the top edge of his paper. "It was...interesting."

*Uh-oh,* she thought. He wasn't pleased. "In what way, Dad?"

He set the paper down and closed his eyes for a long moment. She waited, edgy and breathless, for his critique.

"You let him get the best of you."

*No.* She was sure she had come out on top by the end. "I thought I handled my end pretty well. He's a tough one, Dad."

"I saw that. I also saw something else."

Her breath was trapped in her throat. "What was that?"

"You let him win. You wanted him to."

She shook her head and had trouble finding her voice. "I don't think so."

He nodded. "Yes, you did. You're infatuated with him, aren't you?"

She sat back, deflated. If her father had seen how she felt about Adam, how many of the viewers had noticed? And her producer, had he too seen something in her eyes or heard something in her voice? "I'm not sure 'infatuated' is the right word, Dad."

He folded his hands in his lap, projecting patience. "What is the word, then?"

She couldn't hold his stare. "I'm not really sure. I—I went out with him last Saturday night."

When she told him where they went, he nodded his head in approval. So she decided that was the best tactic to take with him. "He's got a wonderful house over in Formosa. And his office—you ought to see it."

"I know about the man. He's made an impact in the legal community."

"You know him?"

"I know about him. I make it a point to know about all the people my little girl comes in contact with."

Erica felt a suffocating stillness in the room. "Is the air conditioning on?"

"We don't need it."

*I need it,* she thought, but didn't say so.

"Adam Bech is a catch, if that's what you're looking for, honey."

"I'm not sure I'm looking for anyone. I just find him intriguing, that's all."

Parker went back to reading his paper. "Whatever."

She thought of the article she had read about him this afternoon in the office. "There is one problem, though."

The paper didn't come down. Maybe she shouldn't even mention it. Why bother him with the details? Hadn't she already decided for herself that it would be futile to entertain any more thoughts of Adam?

"He has a daughter, Dad."

He set the paper down long enough to tear out an article. "That's nice," he said distractedly.

"No, it's not nice."

He laid the clipping on top of a stack of articles, then frowned at Erica. "Oh, I know you don't need a kid hanging around," he said. "But if this relationship is that important to you, you can work out something with the child. There are always boarding schools."

There were times when Erica lost all sight of who her father was. There were moments—and this was one of them—when he became a virtual stranger.

"I've never actually met her, but I did read an article about her today."

He leaned over and poured another cup of coffee. "What has she done that's worthy of newsprint?"

"It's not what she has done, it's what was done to her. You may remember reading about it in the paper. You see, a year ago, Adam and his wife were having a party on their boat. A Christmas party. There were maybe eight or ten people on board. Some drunk in another boat plowed right into them, the boat engine exploded, and Adam's wife and one of their guests were killed. His daughter was badly burned."

Parker took a sip of the hot coffee and stared at Erica over the rim, saying nothing.

"Do you remember reading about it?" she prodded.

"No. I don't dwell on sordid stories like that."

Erica stayed outwardly calm, but inside she was beginning to squirm under her father's cool scrutiny. "So…"

"So," Parker said, cutting off any chance of an explanation of her disorganized feelings. "That's that, isn't it?"

Erica studied her father's handsome face. She had inherited his looks, or so everyone said. But she wondered now if that was because no one ever looked past her mother's illness to see the woman beneath. Parker never let them.

"I'm not sure it is, Dad."

"What do you mean by that?"

She sighed heavily and shifted in the chair. "There is this program that Larry wants me to do. On boating safety."

"Aha, I see. And you're thinking of using Bech and his daughter as an example."

She closed her eyes. "I wish I'd never seen that article. I can't believe the timing of it all."

"Sounds like great timing to me, honey."

"I'm not sure I could do that, Dad. He's such a nice man. It's like using him or something. And there's this—thing—in his eyes. A hurt. I don't know, I'm afraid that if I mention the idea to him ... I just don't want to add to his problems, that's all."

"Hey." Parker shrugged. "That's business. Sometimes people get hurt in business. Look, Princess, you're no longer interested in the guy now that you know about his daughter, anyway. Are you?"

She shook her head. "No. I don't know."

He held the cup between his hands. "Listen to me carefully, Erica. You do not want to saddle yourself with someone who's got a kid like that. Having a person like that around is a burden, believe me. She'd do nothing but drag you down to her level. Just like your mother did to me." He pointed a finger at her. "Don't even think about letting someone do that to you."

Looking across the table now at the handsome gray-haired man who was her father, at the man who had forged a bond between them that was too strong to break, Erica wished she could truthfully say that what she felt for him was love.

"First of all, Dad, it's not a matter of letting them do that to me. I'm not sure Adam Bech has room for me in his life, anyway."

"Good, then count your lucky stars."

Erica's lips tightened, but she kept any retorts to herself.

"So, what did Larry say when you told him what you were thinking?"

"I haven't. I just found out this afternoon. I wanted to think about it before I mentioned it to him."

"He's going to love it, kiddo. And you've got to concentrate on your career. That is what's important. If Larry'll be gung ho over this idea for the boating segment, then you'd best forge ahead with it."

"I suppose," she said dejectedly.

"There's no 'suppose' to it, Erica. You just do it. That's what is expected of you. Don't let people down now, not after you've made it this far."

She took a drink of coffee and then asked, "Who would I be letting down, Dad?"

He huffed impatiently. "Well, I'd think you'd be letting yourself down." He frowned at her. "What has gotten into you? You were always a winner. You loved being first. Now, I don't know, it's as if you don't even give a damn anymore whether you win or lose."

"Maybe—" she said, hesitating. "Maybe I'm just no longer convinced that not winning is the same as losing."

The disapproving silence that met her from across the coffee table stroked a painfully familiar chord in her memory. Why was she trying to anger her father? Hadn't he done everything for her? He had been the one who had always encouraged her. He had been the one to take her to competition after competition. He had paid for her diction and her singing and her modeling lessons. He had paid for the gorgeous clothes that stood out against the other contestants. He had convinced her that she was a winner. He had done it all.

"I'm sorry, Dad," she said. "And you're right. I need to go ahead with the program. I'm sure it's just a matter of finding the right way to approach Adam about it."

The light of approval came back into her father's eyes. "Good girl." He stood up and moved to the credenza against the wall. "Now, how about a touch of cognac in that coffee?"

"Sure," she said, looking around at the dozens of photographs on the walls. All of her. "Dad, do you have any pictures of Mother?"

He brought the decanter of cognac over to the coffee table. "Why do you ask that?"

"I don't know. I was just curious."

He sat down on the couch, and poured a finger of cognac into each cup. "I may have a few early ones—when we were first married. She was quite attractive back then, you know."

An image of Adam walking down the sidewalk beside a little blond girl came to mind. From the back, she seemed perfect in every way, her little hand held in the grasp of his much larger one. Badly burned, the article had said. What exactly did that mean? She had seen burn victims before, so she could guess as to the extent of the injuries. Months of hospitalization, the article had mentioned. And therapy.

Why did it have to be this way? Why did it have to be Adam Bech's daughter?

Erica's eyes scanned the room once again, and she wondered briefly if Adam Bech had any photographs of his daughter since the accident. Or were they, too, all of a little blond girl who was perfect in every way?

ADAM WOKE UP from another disturbing dream. Swinging his legs off the bed, he sat for a minute with his head cupped in his hands. He glanced up and saw that the hall light was already on. Jilly must have gotten up to go to bathroom and decided to leave it on for him. Just in case. He picked up the clock and stared at the digital readout: 2:15.

A small sound drifted down the hallway. He stood up and followed the sound to his daughter's doorway. Moonlight fell through the window of her room and bathed the bed in its light. She was curled up on her side, a stuffed animal clutched in the curve of her body. The bed covers had been tossed aside. A soft moan escaped from her mouth and she clutched the animal more tightly. With labored steps, Adam walked over to the side of the bed and looked down at the little girl who was haunted by life even in her sleep. He pulled the bedspread and sheet up over her and continued to watch her.

Flashes of another lifetime came to him unbidden, memories of a man who tucked his little girl into bed every night and sang silly songs to her. The one about the frog on the log had been her favorite, but now he could no longer remember the words.

It was a long, slow walk down the lighted hall back to his own room. He stood staring at the big bed, disturbed as the dream came back to him. It hadn't been about the accident. Not this time. His body reacted with a suddenness that frightened him, and he quickly opened his desk drawer and pulled out a pack of cigarettes. The bad habit had almost left him, insinuating itself now only in times of extreme agitation. As the flame from the match flared against the tip of the cigarette, another flame licked through his body.

He didn't want that kind of dream. There was no place for it in his life. He rested his elbow on the tall dresser and took in a deep draw from the cigarette. He'd had them other times since the accident, but not like this one. He could feel the churning deep in the pit of his stomach, the intensity of it eating away at him.

Pushing away from the dresser, he walked into Marilyn's closet and flipped on the light. The long line of dresses hung on the right, while the slacks and blouses and skirts hung on the left. Dozens of shoes were lined up in precise synchronization beneath the color-coordinated outfits.

He smoked faster and harder, deeply disturbed by the wanderings of his subconscious. He had been falling into something soft and leafy, something that smelled of orchids, the bare skin of a woman rubbing against him. The woman was not Marilyn.

Blond hair fell into his face, and the flesh against his hands was pale and hot.

He slammed his hand against the wall and stalked back to the dresser, grabbing the ashtray from the drawer. He ground out the cigarette until it was nothing but ash and broken flakes of tobacco against the bottom of the glass. He closed his eyes and slumped against the wall.

Why couldn't he let go of these desires for Erica Manning? It would go nowhere. He couldn't let it go anywhere. If there was ever to be another woman in his life, it would have to be someone who could accept his daughter completely. Erica Manning would never be able to do that. And it would be unfair to Jilly, having someone like Erica to compare herself to. He couldn't even consider it. He had to stop these dreams immediately. He was having enough trouble getting Erica out of his wakeful thoughts; he certainly didn't want her dominating his dreams, as well. He wasn't even sure he liked her all that much, so why was he dreaming about her?

He was a man obsessed with finding reasons, so he went back to the closet and stared in at all of Marilyn's things. Etta had at one time mentioned boxing them up and giving them to charity, but he hadn't yet found the strength to let her do it. He stood now, looking at the colorful array of fabrics and trying to place Marilyn in the dream. It should have been her, not a virtual stranger like Erica Manning.

He squeezed his eyes shut and tried to recapture the dream, this time with Marilyn's short brown hair and slim, firm body beneath him, over him, surrounding him. The image blurred and he couldn't focus on her face. He tried to imagine each part—her eyes, her nose, her mouth. He tried to form them into a composite, but it wouldn't come. He couldn't get the picture right.

Opening his eyes, he absorbed a reality that he had been artfully dodging for a very long time. In this rare moment of facing the naked truth, Adam realized that Marilyn, his wife of ten years, had become hazy and indistinct to him even before she died.

He flipped off the closet light and went back to bed. The elemental hunger that the dream had wrought in his body had left him. All that remained was a cold emptiness and an awareness of how alone he was.

He thought of the little girl down the hall and wished he could remember the words to the song.

## Chapter Five

It had turned chilly overnight. Not the kind of cold one would expect at Christmastime, but still cooler than it had been in the past few days. Erica hadn't set the alarm, but she woke up early anyway. She had to go into the office today and start working on her next program. Larry was expecting something. Something provocative, something tantalizing.

She stood under the shower spray and tried to feel tantalizing. Giving up, she dressed in corduroy slacks and a heavy cotton sweater. Years ago, she had packed all of her wool away but kept it nearby, hoping beyond reason that the weather would someday call for it. So far, cotton had done the trick quite well.

She had every intention of heading straight for the station but, thirty minutes later, she found herself sitting on a bench in the park on Willow Lane, waiting for Adam Bech to show up with his little girl.

She had no way of knowing for sure whether they would come or not, but something stronger than her reason made her sit there and wait. Despite what her father said, Adam Bech had insinuated himself into her conscious and unconscious mind in a way that had nothing to do with business.

But, now that she was sitting here, she wondered what she would say to him if he did indeed show up. Would she let her emotions rule her entirely, or would she take the practical approach—the one her father had always taken? Was she here to meet his daughter because she cared about Adam, or was she here to meet his daughter to see how she would work for the program?

Despite the cloudy chill in the air, Erica felt perspiration forming at the base of her neck. She rubbed her hands on her pants legs and waited, hoping they would show up soon and wishing they would never come this way.

She saw them in the distance, over a half block away. They were heading toward her, the tall darkhaired father gripping the tiny hand of a small blond girl. As they drew nearer, Erica's chest constricted.

This was business, she tried to convince herself. That was why she was here. She had to look at it that way. She was here for strictly professional concerns. She had a program to do and Adam Bech's daughter could make the difference in the quality of that program. No emotions should come into play.

In the past, they never would have. Erica didn't exist in that kind of world. She lived in a world that had set goals and strict codes, and the inner workings of a person's psyche had little to do with whether those goals were carried out. That was the way she had been taught.

Funny, but no matter how many ways she tried to tell herself that, the sight of the man and his daughter took her breath and her common sense away.

"Hi," a little voice said.

Erica's eyes had locked with Adam's as the two walked up to her; she'd tried to read the pain in his expression. It took a moment to realize that the girl had said something to her.

She lowered her gaze and her heart began to beat frantically. The little face upturned to hers was bright, with curious light eyes. But it was scarred and flawed, as though distorted by a trick of light.

Erica knew Jilly had been burned in the accident and had sustained injury to her right arm, but she didn't anticipate how much the child's simple, cheerful greeting would touch her. She was aware of Adam standing beside her, stiffly awaiting her response. Struggling to show no reaction, she managed, "Hello."

"What's your name?"

She cleared her throat. "My name is Erica."

"Oh, I'm Jilly. Do you live on this street."

"No. I'm—a friend of your father's."

Jilly looked up at Adam's chiseled expression, then back at Erica. "Are you going to the movie with us?"

"No," Adam answered sharply.

"No." Erica smiled. "I'm just here to talk to your dad for a few minutes."

"You're pretty."

Erica frantically looked to Adam for help, but he offered none. He stood there stiffly, almost as if he were daring her to maintain her composure. "Thank you," she said, but her voice sounded weak and insubstantial.

Jilly looked up at Adam. "Will you swing me, Daddy?"

"Sure, baby, just go play for a couple of minutes, okay?"

"Okay." She darted off and Erica watched Adam's gaze follow his little girl.

When he turned back to Erica, his eyes had darkened like the cold sky. "What are you doing here?"

She wanted to stand up and move closer to him. He looked so strong and commanding in his slacks and brown sweater.

"I wanted to see you."

He didn't want to hear that. The dream from last night was still too fresh and real in his mind. But he wanted it to stay that, just a dream, not reality. But God, she looked beautiful this morning. The sweater she was wearing brought out the blue in her eyes and the pants she wore molded her body perfectly. There was nothing about Erica Manning's looks that was not perfect. He couldn't find a single flaw.

"Why?" he forced himself to ask.

"Will you sit down?"

He glanced over toward his daughter. She was running around in circles, pushing the merry-go-round.

"We can go over there, if you want," Erica suggested. "That way you can keep an eye on her."

"Yeah, okay."

Erica stood up and walked beside Adam over to the sandbox. They sat down on the ledge that surrounded it.

"Did you watch the program?"

"No."

She held the disappointment in.

He looked at her and saw it. "I told you, Erica, I don't watch daytime television."

"Not even when you're on it?"

He smiled. "Especially not then."

She smiled back. "Well, it was good. We got some great response on it."

"I'm glad."

"Of course, as my director pointed out, most of the response was from women viewers. You made quite a hit, it seems."

He grinned, looking embarrassed, and shrugged.

"Looks like I've got some competition."

He glanced at her, surprised by her frankness and a bit confused.

She jabbed him lightly in the side. "Don't look so surprised. You knew it all along."

So, Erica was as interested in him as he was in her. God, how long had it been since he'd played these kinds of games with women! Forever, it seemed. Did he still have it in him to do it? And did he even want to?

Erica was looking toward the merry-go-round, toward his daughter, and her smile vanished, answering the question for him. No, he didn't want to play the games.

She looked at him. "I'm sorry about your daughter."

His mouth thinned. "I don't want to hear that."

What was she supposed to say to this man? she wondered. She felt totally inadequate around him. Unequipped, unsure. This was not her. She always knew the right thing to say and when to say it. But with Adam, she was at a loss.

"You're a good father," she finally offered.

He looked away. "A good father would hold her and tell her it will be okay," he said quietly. "But I don't know how to lie to her."

A painful lump formed inside of her and wouldn't go away. This was not what she wanted. Her life was going okay. She had a good job, the possibility of her own show. She was just starting on the climb up. She didn't need this.

"She's very friendly."

Sitting beside her, Adam watched the dazed look in her eyes. Most people were like that around him. He didn't try to help her out of it. He didn't even want her here. She made him feel things he didn't want to feel. He knew it was just physical, a rebellious need that had decided to manifest itself at this particular time and place. As he looked at Erica Manning, it was hard not to feel certain things. It was simply sex, a natural male urge for a beautiful female. And it would go away...

"She's very trusting," he finally said.

Erica braced herself, repeating in her mind the *real* reason she was here. The reason Larry had given her. The reason her father had given her. That was what she had to focus on. She sighed. "There is another reason I'm here."

Somehow, he had known. And, while he knew he should be glad, it made him feel like a fool.

"I didn't think Miss Americas were supposed to look like you," he said, fighting the feelings with a verbal attack.

"How's that?"

He shook his head and answered gruffly, "Never mind."

She could tell by his tone of voice that he had not given her a compliment. And she was baffled. He seemed angry with her for being here, as if she had intruded into her private domain.

"I wasn't Miss America."

"Oh, what was it then, Miss World? Miss Universe?"

She steeled herself against the sarcasm. "I wanted to talk to you about a program I'm doing—a program on boating safety."

He stared at her for a long moment, stunned, and then a disbelieving chortle came from his throat. "I see. Well, Erica, I'll tell you—boating isn't safe. End of story."

"It's an important issue," she said, reaching for his arm when he started to rise.

"Says who?"

"My director. The people who are helping me to work on this story."

"Who gave you permission to delve into my private affairs? Who gave you the right to check into my life?"

"It was an accident, actually. I was researching the Tobias case, hoping I could find something that we missed the other day. A background check on you was part of it."

"I see."

"An article from the paper on the—the accident came up."

"So you decided to exploit it for all it's worth, right? Not enough dirty laundry in city hall these days, so you're going to air mine, is that it?"

"Please, Adam, this is difficult for me. Don't make it harder."

"Hard," he said with a smirk.

"Yes."

"For you."

She swallowed. "Yes."

He shook his head in disbelief. "You can sit here and look at my daughter and tell me that it is hard for *you*. You don't know what hard is, Miss Manning. You don't know the meaning of the word." He glanced over to make sure that Jilly was out of earshot. She was weaving in and out of the monkey bars. "You want me to tell you what hard is? Hard is waking up that little girl every morning and convincing myself that she really does have a life ahead of her. Hard is looking at her across from me at the breakfast table and knowing that I did that to her. Knowing that because of me she will have to live with those scars for the rest of her life. Hard is forcing myself to go on because she needs me, when what I really want to do is find the deepest hole somewhere and crawl into it. Hard, Erica, is living in hell."

*Oh, Erica, don't let it show! Don't show him what his words are doing to you!* "My audience can learn something from this, an important lesson. If—if your daughter came on the program."

He stood stock-still, as if he had been struck. Pain spread like a grass fire through his bloodstream. His eyes lost their focus and then slowly came back on her with blazing intensity. His voice was a furious whisper. "You want my daughter to go on television?"

Erica's resolve wavered for a moment. "Yes, to—to show the results of unsafe boating."

"Go to hell."

She felt as if she had been struck in the midsection, but she had come too far to back down now. If she did, it would mean defeat. She reached out and touched his arm, but he yanked it back as if from the strike of a venomous snake.

"You talked about the rights of parents to protect their children, Adam, but who is it really that you're protecting?"

His voice was a low growl. "I'm saving my daughter from manipulators like you. I'll stop at nothing to do that, you can be assured of that."

"Could I at least ask Jilly if she'd like to do the program? She might, you know."

"I am her father and I am telling you no."

"But if she could help other people, make them think. A drunken boater ran into your boat, Adam. Don't you think that would make people stop and think?"

"Trash journalism, Manning. That's all you're after."

"That's not true. I'm talking about a community service."

Adam saw a couple of boys running down the sidewalk toward the park. They darted around the bicycle rack and up to the swings. He looked at his watch. Why were they here so early? "I'm leaving now, Erica. And I'm taking my daughter with me."

"Will you think about it? Will you let me tell you what I have in mind, how I want to approach this?"

He had the dazed look of a boxer who had reached the seventh round and knew that, for him, it was over. He looked at Jilly on the monkey bars, then back at Erica, and his voice was very tired. "I don't want to talk to anyone. Can you understand that?"

She started to reach for his arm again, but he stood up.

"Especially," he added reluctantly, "not to you."

Something quickened inside her. "Why not?"

He saw the boys heading over to the monkey bars, and he quickly signaled Jilly to come on.

"Why do you say especially me?" she prodded, needing to know.

He looked back at her and hesitated, as if he weren't really sure himself. "Maybe," he finally said. "Maybe it's because you're everything my daughter will never be."

Stunned, she watched the little girl hurry up to her father's side. She smiled at Erica, and Erica searched for the courage to smile back.

She realized, for the first time in her life, that courage was a commodity she had never had.

She walked away, hoping to leave the image of father and daughter behind. But a small voice called out, "Bye, Erica!" And Erica made the mistake of turning around to wave.

"I CANNOT—" Adam threw the rest of his drink down his throat "—I cannot believe the—the gall of that woman!"

Dub reached for the decanter and poured Adam another Scotch. The window behind Adam's head framed a pale moon against a dark sky. "She's a journalist. Ambitious. Concerned with ratings. They love to capitalize on misfortune." He took a sip of his own drink. "The smuttier and grittier the better. They eat it for breakfast. You should know that after all the years hanging around the county courts."

"But to ask me to bring Jilly on the show!" Adam's fingers squeezed the glass, while Dub watched and hoped that it wouldn't break. Mo was partial to her Waterford.

He patted his friend's shoulder. "Relax, buddy. Hope you told her to take a flying leap."

Adam took a drink and tried to remember exactly what it was he had said to her. All he remembered was that he had been operating on some primal level, a condition he didn't like. Every time he was around her, his hormones hit overdrive. He kept getting the signals mixed up. Did he like her or not? Did he want to walk away, or did he want to drag her into his arms?

Confirming once again that he was a mind reader, Dub nonchalantly asked, "So when are you going to invite some lovely lady over here for dinner with us?"

The thought brought a kind of terror to Adam's eyes, terror that dating was expected of him. And terror that Dub might know how he felt about Erica Manning. "I'm not interested in dating. You should know that."

"The softness of a woman can sometimes help. If only temporarily."

"Softness is often an act. I don't need it."

Dub took a thoughtful drink and said, "Whatever you say. But if you change your mind, Mo and I would always welcome the company of any lady you chose to bring over."

Adam scoffed at that. "You really think Mo would accept another woman in Marilyn's shoes?"

"Mo was like a big sister to Marilyn, you and I both know that. But my wife is a realistic woman. She knows that Marilyn is gone. And she knows that you need someone in your life."

"I have someone."

"I don't mean a child. I mean a woman."

Images of a warm autumn morning in the park and a dark night in the hallway of her town house and the blue of a sweater on a chilly morning all rushed down upon him, but he tried to reject the visions as quickly as they came.

"You know," said Dub, thinking, "if Parker Manning's daughter is anything like her old man, she won't let this thing drop."

"Then I'll file an injunction against her."

Dub chuckled lightly at Adam, then saw the serious expression on his face. "Have you ever thought that maybe you're taking this protective thing too far? Maybe that's not what Jilly wants or needs."

Adam scowled. "That's basically what she said."

"Who?"

Adam sighed impatiently. "Her. Erica Manning."

A look of respect came into Dub's eyes. "She said that to you?"

"She asked me who I was protecting."

"And what did you say?"

Adam shook his head. "I don't remember."

"Who *are* you protecting, Adam?"

He was suddenly very tired, as if the room were pressing down on him. He sighed and took a long drink of Scotch. "I always thought I had it in my power to define my own perfect little world. I had it all, Dub. Wife, daughter, career, house, success, friends, everything I needed in life. I thought I could make it perfect, make it all happen." He looked at Dub and shook his head. "I was wrong, wasn't I? It's impossible to do that. All those basic, fundamental beliefs I had were wrong."

"We all believe that, Adam. That is, until we learn—and sometimes in a very tragic way—that life creates its own reality. Not always compatible with what one wants or tries to make it."

Adam finished his drink and set down the glass. He looked at his friend and attempted a smile. "We're a hell of a pair, aren't we?"

Dub chuckled and stood up, slapping Adam on the back. "That we are, my friend. Now, let's go see what Mo has cooked up for dinner, shall we?"

The two men left the oak-paneled study and passed by the living room.

"Look at that," said Dub.

In one corner of the room was a massive Christmas tree, with tiny lights that flickered and reflected against crystal prisms. Jilly was just reaching out to finger a tiny glass angel that hung from a piece of gold thread.

"Don't touch, Jilly," Adam called out sternly. "Just look."

She jerked her hand back and turned around, guilt widening her round eyes.

"Oh, phooey!" said Dub. "I hate Christmas trees that you can't touch. Everything on that is meant to be played with, and it's certainly all replaceable. You go ahead, Jilly-girl, and touch everything on there."

Jilly smiled at Dub, but looked to her father for approval.

"Well, if Dub says it's all right."

She turned back to the tree and again reached out with her left hand for the glass angel. With her back to him, Adam could almost believe that she was normal. That she was his own beautiful little angel, the one who would crawl into his lap at night with a bedtime book. Frowning now, he tried to remember the last time he had read a book to her. He couldn't.

The two men moved on into the kitchen where Mo was putting the last-minute touches on dinner.

"We're going to do this real casual tonight, Adam," she said as she kissed his cheek and handed him a platter with the brisket on it. "I asked Jilly if she'd rather have twice-baked potatoes or macaroni and cheese. She opted for the macaroni. So—" She handed the bowl to her husband. "You fellows can set those on the table for me. By the way, Adam," she said before he left the kitchen. "You haven't given us any ideas yet. What does Jilly want for Christmas?"

Adam stared at Mo for a long moment, then pushed open the swinging door into the dining room. "Nothing."

Mo and Dub exchanged a worried look, then followed Adam. "Hasn't she written her letter to Santa yet?" she asked.

Adam set the platter down in the center of the table and looked at his two friends. "We're not having Christmas this year."

"Not having it!" exclaimed Dub.

"Not having it!" Mo echoed. "You can't stop Christmas, Adam. It comes regardless."

Perturbed, Adam argued, "Okay, Mo, if you want to play semantics with me, then I'll rephrase it. We're not *celebrating* Christmas this year."

"We, as in you and Jilly, made this decision?" she snapped angrily. "Or just you, Adam?"

Adam loved Mo. And she and Marilyn had been like sisters to each other, but he didn't need any didactic sermon from her right now. "We don't need fantasy, thanks all the same."

Mo shook her head. "Maybe that is just what you need."

Adam stood with his hands gripping the back of a dining chair and thought of the fantasy that had been forming in his head for the past week. He wondered what Mo would say if Erica Manning was sitting next to him at her dining table tonight. Fantasies had a way of not working out in the real world.

He forced a calming breath. "Should I call Jilly to dinner now?"

The couple exchanged another glance and Dub said somewhat sadly, "Sure, Adam. Call Jilly."

## Chapter Six

Erica fidgeted in the gray leather chair, struggling to clip the tiny microphone onto the collar of her mauve silk shirtwaist. She did this all the time, so why was she having so much trouble with it today? "If you screw up the angles the way you did last week, Marty, I'll clobber you."

The cameraman peeked a startled face around his equipment. "What are you talking about, Erica? You looked gorgeous . . . as always."

She finally had the microphone clipped on right and let her hands drop wearily to her lap. "I looked like a sick cow. Washed-out. Old."

Marty took retreat behind the camera and tossed the boom operator a what-the-hell's-eating-her shrug. Then he readjusted the angle on her face, a face that could stop traffic on a six-lane highway. Blond hair, creamy complexion, pale blue eyes and a smile that could impair a man for life. A sick cow? Hardly.

"Aren't we touchy today," teased Larry as he hurried with a clipboard across the stage.

Erica glowered at him and snapped at the lighting technician. "Put more pink on me, Al." She fussed with her hair until the hairstylist had to come back on stage and rework his creation. "Touchy," she mumbled under her breath. "I'm not the least bit touchy." She looked at the hairstylist. "Do my lines show? Do I need more makeup?"

He bent down to examine Erica. "What lines?"

Exasperated, she pointed to her face. "These. Around my eyes. Oh, forget it," she snapped. "Let's just get this over with."

She closed her eyes and tried to even out her breathing. What on earth was the matter with her? Why did she feel as if she were clinging to the side of a cliff and that her hands were slipping?

Oh, she knew. It was him. Adam. She couldn't stop thinking about him. Or his daughter. She kept wondering what their life was like, kept picturing them doing the little things together. Setting the table, watching television, cleaning out the garage. It was as if she were obsessed with them, but she knew that was positively ridiculous. She couldn't fathom what the attraction was.

Yes, he was gorgeous. And yes, on the physical level, there were feelings inside of her that wouldn't go away. But even more than that, she wanted to know what he felt about things. She wanted to see inside him, to feel his smile on her when he spoke.

She had dreamed about him two nights in a row. She saw him on every street corner. She ravaged the newspaper, looking for any small article that might contain his name. She didn't want to be this way. This simply wasn't like her.

She had wanted to get away from him and from his daughter the other day in the park; she had wanted to run as fast as she could. She didn't need that kind of problem in her life. But there was this—this anger inside her that wouldn't go away. And it was all directed at herself. The fact that she didn't want to stay—that's what made her so mad. A decent human being would not have felt the way she did. An unselfish person wouldn't have minded that the man had a less than perfect child. A person with any kind of heart or goodness in them would have been able to overlook the little girl's impairment.

But it was there, at the forefront of her mind. And it wouldn't go away. The idea of it all scared her to death. She didn't have time for imperfection. There was no room for it in her life. And, after all, there were plenty of men out there who would fall all over themselves to be near her if she gave them any encouragement. Erica Manning did not have to chase after a man who was not interested in her, especially one who was already encumbered with a problem like that. There was nothing special about Adam Bech....

Nothing, except that she could not seem to control the strange flutterings that his name or the memory of his voice or his eyes evoked in her. He was just a man, she kept reminding herself. Just an ordinary man.

ERICA, WONDERING what insanity had made her come here today, watched as Adam's housekeeper set a steaming cup of hot chocolate on the kitchen table in front of the girl. "You let that cool a bit now."

Jilly was busy cutting stars out of a foil pie pan. "I will."

Erica continued to watch in silence as the little girl weighted the pan down with her right forearm and held the scissors in her left hand. The plate kept sliding away. The housekeeper reached over and steadied the foil.

Outside, a rhythmic cascade of rain fell, pinging against the gutter as it followed the downspout to the flower bed at the corner wall. Inside, Christmas music played on a tape recorder that sat on the counter.

"That's Raffi," said Jilly, pointing to the cassette player. "He's my favorite. What's yours?"

Erica knew what some of her favorite Christmas songs were now, but she wished she could remember the ones she had liked as a little girl. "I like 'Rudolph the Red-Nosed Reindeer.' "

"Yeah, that one's okay, I guess. At school we heard, 'I Saw Mommy Kissing Santa Claus.' " She grinned mischievously. "I know what that means, do you?"

Erica couldn't help but smile. "You're a pretty smart little kid, aren't you?"

"I make straight A's."

"I'm not surprised."

"Did you make straight A's when you were in school?"

"Not always."

"Did you get grounded?"

Erica thought for a minute. "I don't think I ever got grounded."

Jilly sat up straighter and smiled at her. "Me, neither. We're a lot alike, aren't we?"

Erica's gaze flickered to the housekeeper. Etta set a cup of tea before Erica. "I get your program quite often on the telly," Etta said, tactfully changing the subject. "It's rather good."

"Thank you." Erica surveyed the cool airy kitchen, with its flowered tile countertops and copper-colored Mexican tile floor. It was clean and spacious, a reflection of both the woman who had designed it—Adam's wife, presumably—and the woman who now kept it so spotless.

"Do you have to talk business with my daddy again?" asked Jilly.

"Well," said Erica. "Actually I came to talk to you."

"Really? I like company. We never have any, 'cause Daddy doesn't like to, but I do."

"Drink your chocolate now, Jilly-girl, and do your cutouts," said Etta. "Mr. Bech is a busy man," she explained to Erica. "He doesn't have much time for guests."

"I understand." She watched Jilly concentrating so hard on getting her stars right. Just being around the child made her feel inadequate and incomplete. Everything about her spoke of courage and strength and a love of life. But how could that be? Here Erica was, so beautiful by the world's standards, unblemished and unmarred, yet her courage was based solely on everyone's expectations of her. But not Jilly. She seemed confident in who she was. Flawed or not, she seemed to think she was just right.

Erica had tried to talk to her away from her father. Two days ago, she went to the girl's school, but the headmaster had refused to allow the visit. Today she had decided to come to the house before Adam came home from work. She had it all planned out, exactly what she would say to talk Jilly into doing the program. But now, now that she was here, she couldn't do it. Regardless of what her father said or what Larry said, this was wrong. It was exploitation. It was, as Adam had said, trash journalism. This was not simply a medical curiosity or a result of negligence they were dealing with; this was a human being. A seven-year-old bundle of goodness and enthusiasm and raw courage and, as much as Erica knew it was expected of her, she simply could not do it.

"Did you go to the movie last Saturday?" she asked the little girl.

"Yeah, but I dropped my Milk Duds all over the floor. They stuck to Daddy's shoes when he stood up. Do you have a mommy and daddy?"

"I have a dad."

She expected Jilly to ask where Erica's mother was, but, surprisingly, the girl went back to working on her stars.

It was obvious that cutting out the small stars was not an easy task for the child, but Jilly more than endured, she enjoyed. Diligently she worked on her decorations, all the time smiling brightly, her eyes glittering with anticipation of the holiday.

Again Erica was struck by the child's innate goodness, her easy, likable manner... and her acceptance of her impairment. *Face it, Erica,* she thought. *This kid's getting to you.*

She set the cup in the saucer, realizing she had to get away from here as quickly as possible. It had been a mistake to come. It was a mistake to even entertain any thoughts of Adam Bech. It was a mistake to become friends with his daughter.

"Thank you for the tea," she said, standing. "But I—I really need to be heading on."

"I thought you came to visit me," said Jilly, holding up the star she had worked so hard on.

"Yes, I—but I just remembered I have an appointment and—"

"You should stay. Daddy might bring home a Christmas tree. You could help us decorate it."

"Now, now," said Etta, "y'know it's raining." She glanced at Erica with a silent look that spoke volumes. It was patently clear that Etta had given excuses before, and Erica had no trouble reading the sadness in her eyes. Adam Bech obviously had no intention of coming home with a Christmas tree.

"Yeah," said Jilly. "I wouldn't want him to get wet."

With muscles taut as bow strings, Erica turned away "I really have to go."

But before she could make her escape, a key turned in the back door and Adam Bech stepped into the kitchen. He looked very tired. And very wet.

When his eyes landed on Erica, standing only a couple of feet from his daughter, his look turned to fury.

"Hi, Daddy." Jilly held up a foil star. "Look what I made for our Christmas tree."

Adam tried to focus on his daughter and the cutout, but his deadly gaze returned again to Erica. "What are you doing here?"

"She came to see me, Daddy. She's my best friend."

Adam and Erica both turned stunned eyes on the child. Erica felt something inside of her crumble, a wall came crashing in, hurting her, and an unseen hand reached out to pull her away. She couldn't move. Never in her life had she ever been anyone's best friend. Amidst all the competition there hadn't been any room or time for friendship. But here was a child she knew only a few days—the child she had come here to exploit—calling her her best friend. Erica felt touched to her very core. And the father was stunned beyond belief.

"Can I get you a cup of tea, sir?" asked Etta, sensing that now would be a good time to jump in with a diversion. Her employer didn't look so happy right now, and she had a feeling it was all on account of Miss Manning. "Have a seat here, sir, with your little one. She's been working so hard on these stars."

Adam reached over and picked up one of the stars and examined it, though his ability to think had ceased to function. The last thing he expected when he walked in the door was to find Erica Manning. She had invaded his dreams, his Saturday mornings at the park, his privacy, his history and now his home.

"Pretty," he managed to say to Jilly, but his smile was strained. He stared at the star, then set it back onto the table saying, "I'm sure Miss Manning could use this. She can tape it to her office door—just in case she needs a reminder that she's really not mortal like the rest of us."

Startled silence filled the large airy kitchen.

Etta began to clear away the cut foil. "Jilly-girl, I think we need to clean up a bit now and take all this up to your room."

Jilly looked up sadly at Erica. "I guess you'll be gone when I come back down."

"She'll be gone," said Adam before Erica could speak for herself.

Etta led the girl from the room. "Bye, Erica," said Jilly. "I hope you'll come back."

A pain in the back of Erica's throat made it difficult to speak. "Goodbye, Jilly."

For several seconds after they were alone, the room echoed with tense silence. Finally Adam spoke. "I asked you what you are doing here."

She turned to face him and lifted her chin, refusing to be intimidated by him even though his daughter's inner fortitude scared her to death. "You filed an injunction against me."

"You went to my daughter's school."

She swallowed hard, looking for strength. "I—I wanted to talk to her."

"You defied my orders." He shook his head in disbelief. "You went to her school, for God's sake!"

"I didn't get to see her. The headmaster wouldn't let me."

"It's a damn good thing, too, or he'd be looking for a new job."

Erica had so hoped to get out of the house before Adam came home. She had wanted to talk Jilly into coming on the show and then leave. Now everything had gone wrong. Coming face-to-face with the child had changed her mind... again. And now Adam was home. Wet, angry and devastatingly handsome. She could smell the rain on him and the scent of chilled air. It was the first time she had felt that the longed-for winter might actually be upon them. He brushed his fingers through his damp hair, and a droplet of water trickled down his neck, disappearing beneath the collar of his suit coat. He was wearing somber gray, a color that matched almost perfectly the color and mood of his eyes.

"You defied the injunction. I could have you arrested, you know."

Her chin lifted higher. "You could."

The debate warred across his face. "Before I toss you out the door, I want to know exactly what you said to my daughter."

"Why don't you ask her?"

"I'm asking you."

She sighed. "I didn't say anything."

"Yeah, I'll just bet."

"We talked about whether you would bring home a Christmas tree."

Adam took a step backward. He spun away from her and took off his jacket, draping it over one of the kitchen chairs. His hands rested there momentarily, his head down. He took a deep breath. "I'd like for you to leave now, Erica. Please."

Her feet started to move. She wanted to make a quick escape. But, even more, she wanted to stay and let him know how she felt.

"Not until I can apologize," she said, surprising even herself. Erica Manning didn't apologize to anyone. She didn't have to.

He looked up. "For what?"

She had the urge to step up to him and lay her hand on his arm, but she held back, fearing the rejection she knew would come. "For trying to use you. And your daughter."

"That's your job. You use people all the time."

She thought of the little girl working so hard to cut out stars for a tree she wouldn't have. "I was wrong, Adam."

For two days he had despised her. When he learned that she had gone to Jilly's school and tried to worm her way in, he had despised her. And now, here she was, standing in his kitchen, looking more beautiful than any woman he had ever seen. That mass of blond hair framing those angelic blue eyes. Her soft, lilting voice calling his name. How could she look and sound like such an angel, yet at the same time grate on his nerves like the scrape of a fingernail on a dry blackboard?

"You have got to be the most invasive, manipulative, ambitious person I have ever met. You're egotistical and—and . . ."

She stepped up close to him, and he suddenly found it hard to catch his breath. "And what?" she asked, arousing him with her soft voice, making him forget all the words he had in mind for her. Behind him, some guy on the tape player was singing about Papa Noël. How could anyone think straight when someone sang in French?

"And what?" she asked again. "Come on, Adam, surely you can find a few more choice epithets to fling at me. Anything to keep from hearing me apologize, right?"

He was backed against the counter and she was standing much too close. He could smell her perfume. The anger left him as quickly as it had appeared. She drained him, making him realize how empty his life sometimes seemed. When he spoke, his voice was very tired. "I think we've said about all we have to say to each other."

"Not everything, Adam. I haven't said the words 'I'm sorry.'"

If this were one of his dreams, he would reach out and pull her to him, absorbing her body as an integral part of his. His hands would roam urgently over her, touching every square inch, and her eager moans would fill the air around them.

But this was not a dream. This was reality.

He lifted his hand to the back of his neck and tried to massage the tension away. "Tell me, Erica, does your apology change anything?"

"No," she said quietly. "But meeting Jilly does."

His brows drew together. The man on the tape behind him was now singing in English, but Adam still didn't understand what was happening any better than before.

"She's a very special little girl," she said. When he didn't respond, she added, "And she likes me, Adam. Me. Your daughter likes me. And I like her. But I can't fix her, Adam. Is that what you're expecting?"

He folded his arms across his chest. "I don't expect much of anything, Erica. Not anymore. I used to. But all I know is that I have to protect that little girl. I won't allow her to be used. And I won't allow her to go on your program."

They heard the clomp of heavy shoes coming down the stairs. A sense of urgency clutched at him. He should ask Erica to stay for dinner. She was here. All he had to do was ask.

It would be so easy to reach out and touch his arm, she thought. Just to let him know that she was here, that she would stay, that she wasn't going to run away just because his daughter wasn't what he thought the world wanted her to be.

"She's not afraid of the world, Adam," she said quietly.

His throat constricted. He heard Etta opening the front door. "You don't know her."

He was right about that. She knew only what her own life had been like. A pattern had been set long ago. To be with Adam was to break the pattern. Like the breaking of one plate in a set of fine bone china. Some things, perhaps, were not to be tampered with.

"Good night, Mr. B.," Etta hollered from the front hallway.

Reluctantly Adam pushed away from the counter and walked into the other room, saying goodbye to his housekeeper.

When he came back to the kitchen, Erica was gone. He hadn't even heard the back door open and close.

## Chapter Seven

Erica called out from the tiny kitchen. "It's just lasagna that I've had frozen for a while, Dad. Hope that's okay."

From the living room, her father answered. "Sure, honey, whatever you've got. But we can go out, you know."

"I think I'd rather stay home."

He came into the kitchen with a Scotch in his hand. "So, how's the program coming?"

"Well, I've just been doing some research."

"You mean for the program on boating safety?"

Erica slipped the pan of lasagna into the oven. "Yeah," she said unenthusiastically. She went to the refrigerator and pulled out a head of lettuce, an onion and some cherry tomatoes. She carried them over to the counter.

"I thought that was supposed to have run before now," Parker said.

"Well—I've kind of put it off for a bit. I needed time to pull it together."

"But isn't that going to give the other two women a lead?"

Erica shrugged. "Possibly." She began tearing the lettuce apart and dropping the pieces into bowls.

"That's not good, Erica."

She slammed the lettuce head to the counter. "Look, I'm doing the best I can, Dad, okay?" The look of hurt that crossed his face made her immediately regret the remark. "I'm sorry. I didn't mean to snap at you."

He took a drink of his Scotch and, as was his custom, offered no forgiveness.

"It's just that I've needed the time to work this thing out—you know, the problem with Adam."

"You're still seeing him?"

She stared down into the salad bowl and sighed. "Not exactly. I want to, but he hasn't asked, or called, or—anything. I think if there's any asking to be done, it's going to have to come from me."

Parker moved over closer and rested his hand on the counter. "You would actually lower yourself to call a man?"

She regarded him for a long moment. "It's the nineties, Dad. Women do that sort of thing all the time."

"Not you. You've never had to ask for a date in your life."

"Well, to be factual about this, I haven't had all that many dates."

"You didn't need them."

"Says who?"

"You had your future to think of. The pageants, school, a career. I didn't think you were all that interested in men."

"Come on, who are we kidding? I've never known a woman who wasn't interested in men. Oh, I'm not saying a man has to be the priority or anything. But interested in them? Definitely.''

''But we discussed Adam Bech and his—his problem.''

She went back to working on the salad. ''You must be referring to Jilly.''

''Who?''

''His daughter.''

''The handicapped one.''

''If that kid is handicapped, Dad, then the rest of us are hopeless cases.'' Thinking of her, Erica smiled. ''She's an incredible little girl. I've never met anyone quite like her.''

''It's not in your best interest to become involved with them. You can already tell it's affecting your judgment as far as the show is concerned.''

Erica wasn't listening. She was staring at the cherry tomatoes, her knife resting on the counter beside them. ''There's something—something about her that kind of sticks with you. I mean she doesn't look like she feels sorry for herself or anything.''

Parker sighed loudly and shook his head. ''Look, Erica, there are people in this world who are beautiful and people who are not. There are perfect and imperfect ones. Everyone just has to accept what they are.''

Erica regarded her father's face, so calm, so confident that he was right. *Accept that she is imperfect.* Is that what Adam's daughter had done? Or did she see herself differently than other people saw her?

''What did they say about her being on the show?'' Parker's voice had lost all semblance of patience.

''Who? Larry?''

''Yes, and the producer.''

"Well, truthfully, I haven't mentioned it to them yet. I wanted to clear it with Adam first."

"And?"

"And he absolutely refuses to allow it."

"Well, what did you expect, Erica? He has a reputation in this town. He doesn't want the world to see what his daughter is like. It would be embarrassing for him."

Her father's words penetrated, but Erica wasn't sure she heard him correctly. "I don't think it's that at all, Dad." She was having trouble finding her voice. "Do you mean—if I had been like that—if something had happened where I was hurt or disfigured or something, would you want to hide me away?" She knew the answer already. She had seen firsthand what he had done to her mother when she became ill. He had hidden her so that his shame would not be apparent to the world.

"That's a ridiculous question," said Parker. "Go out there to the mirror in the living room and take a look."

"I know what I look like, Dad."

"Then you should know that I would never hide you away."

The long-buried pain clawed its way to the surface of her mind. There were so many memories she had filed away, hoping never to look at again. She had been manipulated by her father all her life and, because of that, there had been so many missed opportunities.

"Adam said I was manipulative," she said, staring dully at the row of cabinets in front of her.

Beside her, Parker beamed. "You can take that as a compliment, dear. Manipulators are people who go after what they want."

She wondered what her father would say if she admitted to him that she had no idea what it was she wanted anymore.

ADAM OPENED THE TOP DRAWER and stared for a long, hesitant moment. Tentatively he reached in and lifted a stack of scarves, setting them on the bed. Next he took a box of belts out and laid them beside the scarves. Without pausing long enough to analyze the import of what he was doing, he began lifting stacks of shorts and T-shirts and tennis outfits, each one spaced carefully on the bed beside the others. When he finished emptying one drawer, he opened the next and followed the same procedure. Within thirty minutes, the dresser was empty.

He stared vacantly at the piles of clothes on the bed, then moved into the closet. Hugging a handful of dresses, he lifted the hangers from the rod and carried the arm load to the bed. They fell atop all the other piles. Moving quickly now and driven by a fierce need to purge himself of the past, Adam hustled back and forth between the closet and the bed, no longer stacking the clothes in neat piles, throwing almost, flinging, desperately trying to rid his life of a pain he couldn't assuage.

An hour later he stood still, staring dully at the mounds of clothes that covered every square inch of his bedroom. Dresses falling off their hangers were sliding to the floor. A jumbled string of mismatched shoes were strewn in a path across the carpeted floor.

He walked over to the corner and sat down in the large chintz chair, his muscles slack, his mind blank. Minutes ticked by as he continued to stare at the jumble of clothes that had belonged to his wife. He had thought before that he should probably do something about them. Give them to some charitable organization. But today, he had raced home from the office in the middle of the day, without forethought, without any plan in mind, and had blindly thrown himself into this frenzied charade. Why today? Why now?

He'd had another dream last night, the kind he shouldn't have, the kind that made him restless all morning and made him think about situations that weren't to be.

He reached for the framed photograph on the table beside him. Somewhat moody hazel eyes in a tanned, well-bred face stared back at him. Marilyn had the look he had wanted in a wife. Sophisticated, cultured, secure. Her clothes had been selected carefully, chosen by the standards of good taste and a reflection of class. Everything she had owned had been chosen in the same way. Her furnishings, her friends. Her husband.

She had chosen him, he knew, selected him out of a crop of young availables. And he had felt so lucky. In all of his wildest dreams, he had never imagined that a woman with the breeding and class of Marilyn O'Donnell would ever have chosen to marry him. He was a nobody. Sure, he was on the rise, full of promise and direction. And college, he knew, had a way of bringing all types of people together. But there she had stood on that afternoon so long ago, in a short skirt and white blouse, on the top step of the Theta House, chattering happily with her friends. Adam had come to the sorority house to work as a busboy in the dining room, and he had fallen in love.

Marilyn had been pretty and vivacious and had sensed in him the things he was to become. She had seen his success long before he had. She plotted it out, pushed him in all the right directions, made it all happen for him. She had been a great asset to his career.

He ran a finger across the face in the photograph. She had been an asset to his personal life, as well. The trouble was, that part of it—the personal part, the loving part—had disappeared so long ago he now had trouble relating to it. The loss had been an intangible thing between them, something neither of them had wanted to admit or face. That would have implied defeat. So they had gone along, year after year, growing silently and inexorably more separate.

But together, they had created a daughter, a beautiful and sweet child that both of them adored. Jilly became the unbreakable link between them, a link that was severed a year ago in one blinding flash of agony.

Adam leaned forward in the chair with his forearms resting on his thighs, the photograph held between his hands. A brisk knock sounded on the door, but it took a moment for it to register in his brain and for him to respond.

"Yes," he said. "Come in."

The door swung wide and Etta stood in the rectangular opening, staring at the chaotic jumble of clothes. As her eyes scanned the piles of clothes, they landed on her employer, hunched over in the chair with the picture of his lovely wife in his hands. If she had let it reach the inner chamber of her heart, she would have cried, but she stopped the scene before it got there. There was work to be done. Mr. Bech needed no more pity added to his own. He needed someone strong like her to take him by the hand and show him the way back from this hell he was living in.

She walked briskly over to the bed and began sorting through the clothes. "You should have told me you were wanting to tidy up the closet, Mr. B. I'll just get these lovelies boxed up and have the church down the street come collect them. They are holding a bazaar next weekend and these things will do quite nicely, I'm sure."

He nodded his head slowly, dazed by her efficiency and no-nonsense manner. She would have made a great legal secretary, he decided.

"Your office telephoned," she went on to say, still rearranging the piles of clothes and picking off the floor the ones that had fallen. "Mr. Grobinski wanted to make sure you hadn't forgotten the meeting with Judge—oh..." She reached into her pocket and pulled out the crumpled piece of paper.

"Judge Eggerton?" Adam said.

"That's it." She read, "'Judge Eggerton.'"

"No," he said, shaking his head. "I hadn't forgotten. What time is it?"

She checked her watch. "It's gettin' on toward half past two."

He was surprised. He hadn't realized how long he'd been home. He had to get back to the office. He had to move. He looked at the photograph in his hands, then at the housekeeper. She was studying him. "Was there something else, Etta?"

She hesitated for only a second. "I was just thinking, Mr. B. I see you with that picture in your hands. And young Jilly was asking me just the other day about her mum and I was telling her this and that.

And she kept asking me all these little things about her. And then I found her up here gazing at that picture. I was just thinking that she might like to have that to look at sometimes. Might like having it in her room, she might."

Sometimes the emotions were so mixed-up inside him that he didn't know how to respond. He wanted to yell and cry and laugh all at the same time. Sometimes he couldn't even identify what it was he was feeling.

He stood up, feeling incredibly old and tired. "Where is Jilly now?"

"She's still at school."

"I—" He glanced down at the photograph. "I think I'll just take this to her room and then I'll head back to work."

"That sounds like a fine plan, sir."

He looked over at the clothes for the last time, knowing that when he came home they would be gone. Forever. Another piece put to rest. "I might be a little late this evening."

"That's all right," Etta said. "I'll fix Jilly a nice supper and wait with her."

He walked to the door, then turned back toward her. "I don't always..." He sighed, unsure of what to say or even of what he meant. "Thank you, Etta."

She didn't show how much his gratitude meant to her. She stood stiffly in the middle of the room and said, "You're a good man, Mr. B. I like doing things for good men."

Adam turned and walked down the hallway to Jilly's room, carrying the framed photograph of the little girl's mother.

JILLY SAT CROSS-LEGGED in the middle of her bed and stared across the room at the picture of her mother that sat atop her dressing table. She fingered her hair and compared it to that of the woman inside the frame. Her mother's short hair was darker and thicker, but she'd always told Jilly that hers would darken as she grew older. She pulled a handful forward and looked sideways, trying to see if it was any darker than it was a year ago. She knew it was shorter. The people in the hospital had had to cut the right side, and when Etta came to see her, she trimmed the other side, too. Now it had grown in some, but it was still short. She didn't mind, she kind of liked it that way.

She stared at the photograph. Her mommy was pretty. She didn't think she much looked like her.

She climbed off the bed and slid her hand between the mattress and box spring. From between the two, she pulled out a wrinkled photograph. She had found it one day in one of the photo albums and had taken it from the book. She had hid it so her daddy wouldn't know she had it. She sat on the floor, her back against the side of the bed, and smiled at the picture in her hand. She didn't know who had taken it, but it was her favorite thing in the whole world. She was between her mommy and daddy, and they were each holding her hands and swinging her. She could almost feel the movement and the air against her face. Cool air, she knew, because they were all wearing sweaters and her feet were dangling just above a big pile of brown leaves. She was little then. Sometimes she wished she was still little.

She folded up the photograph and slipped it back into its secret place. She stood up to get into bed, but her eyes landed on the book she was reading this afternoon. She walked over and picked it up off the floor, shoved her foot into a slipper and bent down to retrieve the other one from inside her doll house.

With book in hand, she padded down the hallway to the closed door. It wasn't really closed, just pulled partly shut, which meant that he was reading or something and hadn't gone to bed yet.

She pushed open the door and peeked around it. He was sitting in the corner chair in stocking feet, glasses slipping slightly down his nose, and he was reading the newspaper. She tiptoed over to the chair and stood beside him. He saw her right away and put the paper down in his lap.

"How come you aren't in bed, honey?" he asked.

She held out the book. "I want you to read me a story."

Adam stared at the book in her hands. It was a standard ritual and really such a simple request, but he felt as if he would rip apart at the seams. It had been too long. Maybe he couldn't do it anymore. The role of father had come so easily to him at one time. But now—now he just didn't know.

He took the book from her hands and looked at it. It was the story of two friends. A frog and a toad. The pages, he saw, were worn at the corners. A much-loved book.

He cleared his throat. *"Frog and Toad Together."*

"Daddy," she said in a small exasperated voice. "I'm supposed to sit on your lap, remember?"

The ritual had begun. He picked up his cue and spoke his lines by rote. He looked at her in feigned surprise. "You are?"

"Of course."

"Oh, well, then I suppose that will be all right."

She sighed the well-rehearsed sigh and crawled up into his lap, pushing the newspaper into a heap on the carpeted floor. She fidgeted until she got comfortable, then said, "Now you may begin."

"May I?"

"You may."

He cleared his throat again. *"Frog and Toad Together."*

"It's upside down, Daddy."

"What is?"

"The book." She giggled and shifted it around in his hands. "See?"

He frowned at the book in his hands. "Well, it's—it's a completely different story this way. I'm not sure I can read it now."

She laughed. "Of course you can. You've read it to me five gillion times."

He had, he knew. But always before it had come naturally. It had been so easy. Sitting here tonight, reading to his little girl, was suddenly one of the hardest things he had ever done in his life. He remembered his lines, and he said all his parts, but the play was not the same. Somebody had turned out the stage lights. The backdrop was all wrong.

When the story ended, she made no move to leave.

"Daddy, how come you don't like Erica?"

He felt a thin line of sweat bead up on his lip. "What makes you say that?"

"You're so grouchy when you see her. I think she's pretty. Don't you think she's pretty?"

His heartbeat sped up. "Yes, I think she's pretty."

"Me, too. I wish she'd come visit me again."

Adam sighed. "I don't want you to count on that, Jilly. I don't think she'll be coming back."

"Really?"

"Really."

Jilly's thumb popped into her mouth and then, remembering she wasn't supposed to do that, she pulled it back out. "Oh," she said, in a voice too calm, too rational. "Okay."

She climbed off his lap. "Night, Daddy."

"Good night, Jilly."

She looked directly at him. "I love you."

He felt the tears pool behind his eyes as he stared at the disfigured little girl standing beside his chair. His throat constricted, and the pain clawed like talons at his chest.

In a hesitant voice, she said, "You're supposed to say 'I love you more.'"

He couldn't. His throat was too tight. The pain had seized him in its iron grip. She was waiting, standing there with that look in her clear hazel eyes—her mother's eyes—waiting for him to say his lines. He swallowed hard and blinked back the tears. "I love you more," he whispered.

She seemed to let go of the breath she had been holding and walked toward the door. "I love you ten times more."

He hesitated, wanting to rub his eyes, but not in front of her. "I—I love you a hundred times more," he croaked.

"I love you a million times more."

His voice faltered. "I love you...infinity times more."

At the doorway, she turned around and grinned. "I love you infinity plus one." And then she was gone.

He could hear her feet shuffling against the carpet as she went back down the hallway to her room. She flipped on the hall light.

*Infinity plus one.*

The floodgates opened and, this time, Adam didn't try to hold it back.

## Chapter Eight

The days until Christmas were numbered. Everyone rushed everywhere: through the malls, in and out of parking lots, to parties and plays. Nothing moved at its normal pace.

Erica stood on the sidewalk outside the station and closed her eyes. She could feel the cold snow hitting her face, the delicious chill over her body. If she stuck out her tongue, she could taste the snow on the tip of it. She could hear the tinkling of bells from the Salvation Army collectors on the street corners.

When she opened her eyes, she noticed that a group of teenagers were staring at her. Their radios blared with the screech of heavy metal. She lifted her hair off the back of her neck to cool it. The air was once again hot, the sky clear.

Okay, she decided, if it's not Currier and Ives she would make it that. She had never bought a Christmas tree for herself before, but this year she was going to do it. It was ridiculous to go year after year, wanting something so desperately and not making it happen.

As long as her wants had been the same as those of her father, life had been easy. Everything had been given to her. But there were other things she needed now, things that no one would give her, things she would have to get for herself.

Skipping lunch, Erica drove out to one of the large Christmas tree lots. The selection was huge. She wondered how anyone ever decided on which tree to buy. Wandering down the long rows, she finally found a Douglas fir that she liked. She paid the man and requested that it be delivered to her address.

She was walking out of the lot when she suddenly remembered Jilly sitting at the kitchen table, cutting out foil stars for a Christmas tree, a Christmas tree they didn't have. Erica stopped, thinking, then slowly continued to walk. It really wasn't any of her business. It was their life. Their decision. But Jilly...oh, how she seemed to long for a Christmas tree. And Erica knew what that was like. Her father had always said they were too much trouble to put up and take down. Her mother had never been well enough to do it. So, as a child, Erica had to content herself with decorations that she made at school.

She thought of Jilly at the kitchen table, and she suddenly saw herself at that age. Just like Jilly. Lonely, needing a mother, needing a father to understand how important traditions were to a child, needing a warm Christmas to make everything better—even if only for a little while.

Erica spun around and dashed back to the lot. There had been another fir, next to the one that she bought, that was equally beautiful. "I'll take it," she told the salesman.

"You want two trees?"

She grinned. "Yes." She pulled the money out of her wallet to pay him.

"And you want it delivered to the same address?"

Her grin wouldn't go away. She couldn't remember when she'd felt so excited about anything. So happy. "No, I want you to strap this to the top of my car."

Dragging the tree behind him, she led him to the car. He stared at the shiny BMW, its paint flawless and glossy. "You sure about this?"

"Positive," she said. "Throw it up there."

"Okay, lady. It's your life."

Smiling contentedly, she silently agreed. Yes, and for the first time, she was living it her own way.

ADAM PICKED JILLY up from school that afternoon because Etta had a dentist's appointment. They drove into the driveway, and he heard his daughter's squeal of delight before he saw the reason for it. Before he could turn off the engine, she had bounded from the car, her backpack flapping against her side as she ran up to the house.

Propped against the shrubs to the side of the door was a large tree. Adam stooped to pick up Jilly's backpack where she had dropped it on the steps. He came up beside her, feeling a sense of dread inside of him.

"A tree, Daddy! A Christmas tree! I knew you wouldn't forget. I just knew it!"

Adam stood mute beside her and stared at the perfect tree. Had Dub bought this? Or had someone else?

"Look, Daddy, here's a letter from somebody."

From a red ribbon tied to a center branch, a card hung. His heart beat too rapidly in his chest as he saw Jilly reach for the card. Over her shoulders, he saw the handwriting—feminine, stylish, written with a flourish. Not Mo's handwriting. And certainly not Dub's.

"It's in cursive, Daddy. But it says me. See right there."

He took the card. "'For Jilly,'" he read, his pulse pounding in his ears. "'From a friend.'"

The little girl reached out in awe and gingerly touched the tree, sighing contentedly. "A friend."

Adam wanted to be angry. He searched inside himself for the emotions he knew should be there. But all he found was a sense of wonder. And longing.

He glanced at Jilly. It had been a long time since he'd seen that look of pure happiness and joy on her face. Something hard and too-long frozen inside him began to thaw. "Guess we'd better get this inside and put some water on it."

She threw her arms around his waist and hugged him tight. "I love you, Daddy. It's going to be a good Christmas, isn't it?"

He smiled down at her, holding inside the painful memories of the last one they had known. "Yes, honey," he said softly. "It's going to be the best."

ADAM'S HEELS CLICKED along the tile corridor of the television station. He would have felt conspicuous if it hadn't been for all the other people clicking and clacking their way in and out of offices, some rushing with last-minute scripts to the soundstage, others dashing back to answer ringing telephones.

He stopped twice and asked directions, then continued on his way. When he had come for the interview two weeks ago, he had been led directly to the taping studio. He had never been to Erica's office before.

*Erica.* He still couldn't even think her name without causing a turmoil inside his body. Just when he thought he could justify not liking her, she turned around and did something to make his little girl smile. But still, he couldn't entirely rid his mind of the thought that maybe—just maybe she was doing this for a reason. Was it possible that she was trying to buy Jilly's friendship? That all she wanted was for Jilly to appear on her program? His fists clenched at his sides as the thought pierced through him. He had to know. He had to find out the truth. For himself, as well as for his daughter.

He could no longer deny the hold she had over him. The content of his dreams had changed entirely. He still had the nightmares, but they were usually combined with others that were sensual and maddeningly erotic. It was his hands on her skin, his mouth dueling in a hot debate with hers, his fingers inside her moist body, her arms wrapped tightly around him. Guilt consumed him, yet he couldn't make the dreams end. And, as much as he wanted to, he couldn't stay away. He had to see her. Just this once, he told himself.

He turned left down the corridor where the news offices supposedly were. A maze of half-walled cubicles filled a large room. As he drew nearer, he heard her voice, soft but with a defensive edge to it. Her voice, spiraling through him like liquid fire.

Another man was with her, talking now, so he hung back, not wanting to interrupt.

"And I'm getting fed up," Adam heard the man say. "I've been patient with you. I've defended you on every front."

"I know that, Larry. You know how much I appreciate what you've done for me."

"So why can't you come through with this? We've gone over the content. You were excited about this segment. You had the problem with the little girl wrapped up, you said. Now you're telling me you can't get her."

Adam took a step backward, his heart pounding, fists curling back into the clench.

"That's right, Larry, I can't."

Adam frowned, but his body didn't yet relax.

"But why? What's the problem?"

"The problem is it's wrong. She doesn't belong on this show."

"What the hell is that supposed to mean?"

"It's exploitation, Larry."

A full five seconds of silence followed and then, "Am I hearing you right? Am I talking to Erica Manning? You of all people should know the meaning of exploitation. That about sums up your whole life."

Adam felt himself cringe, as if the blow had been directed to him.

"That's unfair," came the soft reply.

"Let me tell you what is unfair, my dear. What is unfair is that I have given you too many chances around here. I have bent over backward for you. Now why, I sure as hell don't know. Maybe I, like everyone else, am so bowled over by your looks that I can't see straight around you. I don't know. All I know is that I've had it. You said you were going to do the boating story. We've got it all set up and slotted. Now, I expect you to follow through and do it."

"Then I'll do it without Jilly Bech."

"Fine," he growled. "You can do it with a walrus for all I care. Just do it!"

Adam hung back as the man—the director he had met two weeks ago—stomped out of the office and thrashed his way down the hall, steam practically rolling from his ears.

Adam moved down the few feet to her office and stopped in the opening to her cubicle. She was sitting at her desk, but she was staring at a painting on the wall. Done in the impressionistic style, it showed a rather plain-looking woman seated for a portrait, but the artist behind the easel was transforming the woman into a goddess.

He looked back at Erica and his pulse quickened. She was a goddess. He had never known any woman more beautiful. And, despite all the misgivings, he knew deep inside that he wanted her in his life. He didn't know where she would fit, but he knew he wanted her there. Somewhere.

She turned, finally, and noticed him standing there.

It took a moment for her to realize that she was looking at Adam Bech and not some fanciful vision she had conjured up.

"How long have you been standing there?" she asked.

"For a bit."

She waited, tense with expectations and confusion. "Then you heard."

He nodded. "I heard." He hesitated, wanting to know the truth but afraid of what it might mean for his own life. "What made you change your mind?"

Her instinctive need for protection made her tense, but she saw the bewilderment in those quiet gray eyes, the need for truth in his face. "I wanted to get it right, Adam. For once in my life."

He came into the office and walked over to her. She was sitting so still, looking up at him, needing something that he wasn't sure he had to give.

He sat down on the edge of her desk and looked at the floor. "You may have picked the wrong man to do that with."

His hands were clasped in front of him and she reached over and rested her fingers lightly against the back of his hand. "I don't think so."

His grip loosened and he took her hand between his, examining her smooth slim fingers. He finally looked up. "Why did you buy the tree?"

Her pulse beat anxiously against his thumb, and she wondered if he had been angry when he saw the tree on his porch. "Because Jilly wanted one, and..." She forged ahead, knowing that her words might anger him. "And because I think you had no intention of buying her one."

His hand closed around her fingers. "You're right. I wasn't going to."

She stood up and tentatively moved closer to him, standing between his spread legs. She reached up and laid her hand against his cheek. It felt warm to the touch. "Lots of people are lonely at Christmas, Adam. We don't have to be, you know."

Looping his arms around her waist, he pulled her close and buried his face in her hair. His eyes closed and he felt himself falling into a warm, protective place, a place where he could hide from the demons that had been confronting him every day for the past year. He knew it was only a temporary fix for all the things that ailed him, but for now that was enough.

He was aware of everywhere her body touched his, and heat began to flood his bloodstream. He held her at arm's length, hoping to instill some sanity into the moment. "I think I'd better get out of here."

She smiled at the expression on his face. "Why don't we go for a walk?"

He looked vastly relieved. "That sounds like a good idea."

THEY FOLLOWED A PATHWAY, shaded by willow and oak, that ran beside the winding bayou. Since leaving her office, they hadn't said much. After the first hesitant steps toward establishing a relationship, neither of them knew what to do next. On the outside, it appeared so simple. A successful lawyer, handsome and well liked in the community, with a journalist, beautiful and successful—they were the perfect blend.

But nothing was as simple as it seemed. Erica had never in her life had to give anything of herself. Everything had always been given to her. She wasn't sure if she had enough inside to give to someone else. And for the past year Adam had been lost in a world for which he was unequipped and unprepared. He had been sinking in a pit of despair for so long, he wasn't sure he knew how to climb out of it. Erica made him want to live again, but he didn't know if there was any life left in him to live.

They were two lost mariners, tossed on the open sea, two explorers who had set sail with the hint of a new world, but also with the possibility of reaching the edge and falling into an abyss from which there was no escape.

He was looking down at the path on which they walked when he finally spoke. "I don't know if I'm ready for this in my life."

"You mean for me?"

He glanced over. "Yes." He saw that she needed an explanation, but he didn't know if he could formulate one that she would understand. "For the past year I feel like my life has been one big battlefield." He stopped and kicked a rock aside, then stared over the slow-moving bayou. "I—I've got these wounded soldiers lying all around me. And I've got no strategy, no battle plan at all. The enemy is closing in, but I can't see it. It's all sneak attacks. And I'm not prepared." He looked back at Erica, her soft eyes absorbing him. "All my life I've been prepared...until this happened."

It was the first time that anyone had ever spoken so intimately to her. She'd had many acquaintances through the years, but she'd never had a friend. Not a real one. Never a confidant. For almost thirty years, she'd only had to think about herself. What were her goals? What were her ambitions? Her assets and strategies. Other people's were of no concern to her.

Until now. This man brought out feelings in her that she'd never had before. With him, she wanted to step outside herself. But when she did, the world looked very different to her, and she wasn't sure how to approach it. She was secure and snug in the one she and her father had created. It was home, a perch on which to roost, an exquisite shell in which to hide any imperfections. She wasn't at all sure she wanted to leave it. Yet with Adam, she seemed to have no choice. With him, she couldn't remain cloistered. With him, she knew she would have to face a very real and sometimes terrifying world.

She finally found the strength to speak. "You might have allies that you didn't realize you had."

He looked dubious. "I don't know. I haven't seen many signs of it. I do have Dub."

"Your partner?"

"Yes. And his wife. They're our best friends."

*Our,* he said. She heard it, and she knew what it meant. Facing the truth, she knew that what she had been most afraid of facing was not Adam's daughter, but his dead wife. *Our best friends.* They'd had a life together. Between them, they created a daughter. They had loved together and planned together. And when she died, something in him had died, too.

"You must miss her very much," she said softly, looking away from him.

Adam hesitated, frowning. "You mean my wife?"

Erica turned toward him. "What was her name?"

"Marilyn."

"You must miss her very much."

He reached out and wrapped his hand around the base of Erica's neck, pulling her close. His other hand came up to rest against her jaw. She knew that he was going to kiss her, and she wondered briefly, in the moment before his lips touched hers, if she was a substitute for the wife that he no longer had.

Her eyes closed when his mouth moved over hers, and she stopped caring why he was kissing her. She was simply glad that he was. He was warm and tender, and she wanted the moment to go on and on forever.

He held her in a long embrace, her cheek leaning against his chest, his chin resting atop her head. "I must sound pretty pathetic to someone like you," he murmured above her.

There it was again. *Someone like you.* The same old refrain she had heard a thousand times. Everyone assumed so much about her. No one could ever believe that her life was not one long carnival ride, full of glee, never empty, never lonely. "You might be surprised to know..."

When she paused, he said, "To know what?"

"Never mind."

He held her at arm's length. "Surprised to know what, Erica?"

She kept looking anywhere but at his face. "My life is not so perfect, Adam. Everyone thinks it is, but it's not. You're not standing here with any great treasure. I mean, guys are not exactly knocking down my door to be with me."

"I would."

Her eyes locked with his. "Would?"

His gaze faltered. "It's a big step for me, Erica. There are so many considerations, so many... problems."

"Do you mean Jilly?"

"I have to be very careful with her, Erica."

"Does that mean you don't want me to get to know her?"

He stepped back and slipped his hands into the pockets of his slacks.

"I don't know."

"Adam, I like her. I think she likes me. Why is that so difficult for you to understand?"

He shook his head. "The contrast would be too painful."

"What contrast?"

He stared at her long and hard. "Between the two of you."

She felt as if she had been slapped hard across the face, and her voice shook when she spoke. "Painful for whom?"

"For Jilly. You're everything she will never be."

"She wasn't bothered by surfaces with me. She wants a friend."

"She has me, and Etta, and Dub and Mo."

"Oh, your nice little insulated world, is that it? A private club where no one else can join. You're the one who's afraid, Adam. Aren't you? You're the one who can't face the comparison."

"That's right," he snapped, kicking another stone off the path. "I can't! Don't you understand that every time I look at you, I see all over again what I've done to Jilly. *Me. I* ruined her life." He sniffed derisively. "But, of course, you couldn't possibly understand that. You have only yourself to worry about." He picked up a long piece of bark and broke it in half. "You don't know what it's like to hold another life in your hands and then to drop it. Just drop it and watch it shatter."

Erica felt as if a steamroller had run over her. She felt bruised and raw, and her nerve endings rattled inside her. He refused to see her at all. He refused to see anything but his own warped vision of the world. He was a man in real pain. She knew that. And she wasn't at all sure she had the strength or the ability to heal him. She was only beginning to learn how to heal herself.

She moved over to the edge of the creek and stared down at the reflection of the trees that lined the bank. Adam remained behind her, hearing a sadness in her voice that he hadn't heard before.

"I remember one time—when I was young," she was saying. "My dad took me to an antique shop. To buy whatever I wanted, so he said. There was this beautiful Chinese vase that he wanted me to get. But I saw this porcelain figure sitting next to it. It was beautiful, except that, at one time, it had broken and been glued back together. I remember the shopkeeper telling us that it had belonged to a large family with a house full of rambunctious kids. One of them had dropped it and it had broken into several pieces."

She turned around and looked at him, her eyes brimming with tears. "I wanted that figurine, Adam. I wanted it so badly. I kept thinking about those rambunctious kids playing with it, caring for it, making up games and fantasies about it. Though it was only porcelain, I could see that it was full of life. And I just knew it had a story to tell."

She turned back around, watching a male and female cardinal dipping down to the bank together to gather twigs for a nest. "My father bought me the vase." After a long pause, she said, "Don't do that to your little girl, Adam."

Adam felt the blood bounding through his veins as he looked at her from behind. He wanted to protect Jilly and keep her safe. He didn't want to keep her from living.

"Is that what I'm doing?" he asked in a painfully quiet voice.

Erica turned around and regarded him for a long moment. "I don't know, Adam. I hope not. She's so full of life. Don't let that part of her shatter, too."

He had thought he would never again be able to think about a woman the way he was thinking about Erica right now. Wanting to touch her. Yearning to wrap her lovely softness inside him, and let it keep him warm and safe. Wanting it, it seemed, more than he'd ever wanted anything in his life.

She stepped up to him and smiled softly. "I don't want to hurt her any more than she's already been hurt, Adam. I just want to get to know her. Will you let me try?"

The walls were crumbling around him, but he struggled to keep them in place. It was too soon! his mind shouted. But the pain inside of him cried equally as loud for release. With Erica Manning standing before him, he saw both solace and hurt. He wanted to believe that it would work, that he could find in her the peace he so desperately needed. But he just didn't know. He was still groping around the center in a darkened room, trying to find his way out. There were too many doorways offering temptations and solutions. Which one? Which one should he believe?

"We can try," he said, taking the first step out of the darkened center.

She leaned against him and sighed.

## Chapter Nine

"So you're really not going to do it."

Erica crossed her arms and tried to shove away the fear that nipped at her heels. "No, Larry, I'm really not."

He stared at her for a long time, then sighed. "It's become real slipshod lately."

"The show?"

"Your work."

The fear gnawed away at her bones. Erica pictured her father, standing in the wings of a stage. She was seven years old. Three other girls were ahead of her in the preliminary competition. Her father's face had flattened into an expression that she, at seven, had had no trouble deciphering.

She had tried even harder that day and, in the finals, she had come out ahead. Number one.

"Just because of the boating segment?" she asked.

He shook his head. "Not just that."

Erica nodded slowly. Another man came into view, and her father receded farther into the background. Adam Bech stood now in the wings of her mind, watching her. She saw him the way he looked today at noon, standing beside the shady bayou. *We can try,* he had said.

A sense of commitment grabbed hold of Erica for the first time in her life. She had a goal of her own, one of her own making. If she won this one, she knew she'd never have to search for another. This would be the end of the struggle. She would finally have the prize she had wanted all along—a family to love and to love her.

She found the strength to look directly at Larry without showing a flicker of doubt. "I'm doing my best," she said clearly. "I'm sorry if it's not good enough."

He was surprised, but he covered it well. "A decision is going to be made next week."

"I see. You mean about who will stay and who will be cut."

"Yes. You could still pull it off, Erica."

Her strength wavered as the familiar self-doubts assailed her. What if Adam didn't want her in his life? What if she failed the tests he set before her? What if she lost him and her job—and her father's approval?

Her gaze lowered to her desk. "I'd like to know how I could pull it off, Larry."

"Well, you've still won the draw for the Christmas show at St. Joan's."

She shrugged. "That's true."

"And that's a lucky break. The audience always loves that one. A Christmas party for hospitalized children is a consistent ratings winner."

"I know."

"Try to come up with something fresh on it. A new angle, okay?"

"I'll try, Larry."

Just before he left, he asked, "You are coming this weekend, aren't you?"

"To what?"

"The station's party. We're all taking the train to Galveston for 'Dickens on the Strand.' You really ought to come. It's going to be great fun."

She had never gone to one of the station's parties before, so she had no intention of going now. They were always rowdy outings with lots of drinking and carousing, filled with people with whom she had nothing in common. She'd probably opt to have lunch with her father instead. But to Larry, she said, "Sounds like fun. I'll have to see what's going on."

When he was gone, Erica stared at the mounds of files on her desk. Options, all of them. Story ideas, news clippings, biographical sketches. All potential subjects for *Focal Point*. With her elbow on the desk, she cupped her chin in the palm of her hand and sighed. Why didn't she care? Why couldn't she get excited about any of these ideas?

She closed her eyes and pictured a dark green pine, its fragrant needles and branches covered with lights and baubles. She wondered if Adam and Jilly would decorate their tree tonight. She wondered if maybe she should drop by and just . . . No.

She picked up one of the files on her desk. This was safer. Here, working, she couldn't fail Adam's test.

ADAM PULLED OPEN a drawer and propped his ankles on it while he leaned back in his chair. "I filed the Motion for Partial Summary Judgment today, but I'll tell you, this thing is going to drag out for years."

Dub lit a cigar and closed his eyes, relishing the first draw. "These pipeline claims usually do."

"The problem is I'm not sure our clients have the money to pursue it that long."

"Have you explained how long it will probably take?"

"Yeah, I've told them."

Dub shrugged. "Then we've done our part. If they want to go ahead with it, then that's their choice."

Companionable silence, forged by many years of working closely together, enveloped the room. This had been their habit for years. Before leaving for home, they'd sit in either Dub's or Adam's office and hash through the day's events, often debating the technicalities of the American legal system.

Tonight Adam was having trouble winding down. His mind was a jumble of contradictions, of wants and dislikes, of needs and anguish.

"Well, I hope you're satisfied," he finally blurted out, none too pleasantly. "We finally got a tree."

Dub drew on the cigar and exhaled slowly, watching Adam. He hadn't failed to notice how anxious he'd been the past few days, reminding Dub very much of a young boy poised on the edge of a high diving board, wanting to jump, longing to be like all the other boys frolicking happily in the water, but scared to death of the fall. "A tree." He smiled. "Well, I'm delighted. Has Jilly loaded it down with all the decorations?"

"Not yet. We got it yesterday, but I couldn't find the decorations. Etta knew where we kept them, of course, and was going to dig them out today." He scowled. "Wouldn't you think I would have known where the decorations were?"

"Shoot no. I don't know where half the stuff in our house goes to hide."

"Well, anyway, decking the halls is on the agenda for tonight."

"Did you get the tree at that lot over there on Gaston?"

Adam dropped his feet to the floor and slammed shut the drawer. "No. It—it was given to us."

"Well, you don't have to glare at me. I didn't do it."

"She did."

"She?"

Adam looked out the window and mumbled, "Erica Manning."

Dub strained to hear. "Erica Manning, did you say?"

"Yes."

Dub sat back and scrutinized his partner. "Erica Manning," he mused, smiling. "She actually brought it over to you, did she?"

"She left it in the front yard."

Dub laughed. "Well, I'll be damned. How about that?"

Adam glared at him again. "Why the hell does that make you so happy?"

Dub puffed on the cigar, and a wreath of smoke encircled him. "Because, old buddy, it's a monkey wrench in the works."

Adam scowled. "What are you talking about?"

"Erica Manning. And her Christmas tree. It's a new complication in your life."

Adam thought of the walk they had taken together today. He thought of the way she had looked in her copper skirt and jacket and with those clear blue eyes, the curve of her mouth so soft and inviting. He thought of the things he had said and the things she had said. He thought of her hand in his, a simple little touch that had him wanting much, much more. He thought about making her a part of his life and wondered if it might just be the biggest mistake of his life.

"And that makes you happy?" he snapped at Dub. "That I have more complications?"

"Of this type, yes."

"What type?"

Dub stubbed out his cigar and stood up, then stretched and patted his stomach. "The male-female kind." He grinned and walked to the door. "See you Monday, old buddy." He stuck his head back in. "Oh, and by the way, Mo's ready for another dinner. You're welcome to bring Miss Manning along. I guess she's not the barracuda you thought she was."

When Adam was alone, the large paneled office grew as still as night. The lingering scent of furniture polish, mingling with the smell of Dub's cigar, filled his nose. Complication? The male-female kind. Her hand, all soft and pale and smaller than his, her flesh touching his, warming him.

But there wasn't just him, he had to remind himself. There was Jilly to think of. He had to be so careful with her, so careful not to expose her to the wrong things in life or to people who would use her and hurt her any more than she had already been hurt.

He thought of the other night, when Jilly had crawled into his lap with the book. Why don't you like Erica? she had asked. I hope she comes and visits me soon.

His eyes squeezed shut. But what did she know? She was a child. She had no concept of how much more badly she could be hurt in this world. She was so trusting, so vulnerable, she would see everyone as good and nice and pretty. She didn't know what could happen. She just didn't know.

Locking up his desk, Adam finally admitted that a good part of his fear was for himself. Jilly he had vowed to protect, and he knew he could. The real question was, could he protect himself?

ERICA HAD PULLED her car into the curb and switched off the engine. She sat for a moment, staring up at the big handsome brick house, skirted with ligustrum and azalea bushes. The house was dark except for a few pale lights through the windows. All the other houses on the block, she noted, were draped with colorful strings of Christmas lights. But not this one. Not Adam's. It gave the impression that the house had been abandoned and that no one had lived here for a long time. She wasn't at all sure she wanted to be here. She didn't need these problems in her life; she had enough of her own to deal with.

And yet she opened the car door and climbed out. She walked slowly up the sidewalk, knowing she was making a big, big mistake, but unable to make herself turn around and go home.

Adam heard the knock and he had the money in his hand when he opened the door. He swung the door wide and stretched out his hand to pay.

Erica looked down at the proffered money. "Has it come to that? You're going to pay me to leave you alone?"

The remark and the tone, she knew, were flip, but it was the only way she could counteract the emotional upheaval that was going on inside of her. It was a jolt to her senses every time she looked at him. He looked great, standing in the doorway, looking relaxed in corduroy slacks and a blue chambray shirt.

Adam pulled back the hand with the money and gripped the edge of the door. "I—I thought you were the pizza boy."

She shrugged. "Sorry. Just a friend." She smiled. "Of course, if you want me to be the pizza boy, I will."

She was here, standing on his doorstep, and Adam couldn't find his breath. She was like a shining jewel that had just been presented to him, a glittering diamond in a delicate setting. She looked terrific standing there in a soft white lamb's-wool sweater and black leather slacks. Gorgeous, in fact. She was too tempting. He wished he had it in him to resist her.

He smiled back. "I kind of like you the way you are." He knew why she was here. She wanted to get to know Jilly. She wanted to get to know him. He had thought of asking her at noon if she wanted to help them decorate the tree, but something had held him back. But she had come anyway, like a surprise package.

Erica heard footsteps coming up the sidewalk behind her. In the periphery of her vision, she saw a boy in a striped hat and shirt standing beside her. The warmth from the box in his hands radiated off him. She looked at the boy and then at Adam. She grinned. "Pizza."

"Large pepperoni and a bottle of Pepsi. That'll be twelve-fifty, sir."

Adam paid the boy and took the warm box, holding it awkwardly in his hands, balancing the bottle on top of it.

"I—I've got to set this down—in the kitchen."

"Okay," Erica said. "I won't sneak in and steal all your silver while you're in the kitchen. I'll wait right here."

Feeling like an idiot, he pulled the door wider. "Come on in."

She smiled. "Thanks." She took the Pepsi from the top of the box and followed him to the kitchen.

Jilly was seated at the kitchen table, and with her left hand was trying to trace a map of the United States from a big world atlas. When she saw Erica, she gasped softly. "You came back to see me!"

Erica and Adam shared a quick glance. Erica tried to still the racing of her heart as she smiled at the girl. "Yes, I did."

The little girl looked at her father to gauge his reaction. "I told Daddy I hoped you would. Are you eating pizza with us? Are you going to help us decorate our tree?"

Again Erica looked at Adam and saw the indecision wavering in his eyes and at the corners of his mouth. "You're welcome to stay," he mumbled, refusing to look directly at her.

Her own doubts surfaced, but she shoved them back down. After all, she had come here to see him and Jilly. She had come here for this very reason. After the agonizing she had done while driving over here, why should she back out now?

"I'd love to." She looked from the eager face of the child to the worried face of the father and she thought, *What am I getting into?*

Adam turned his back on her, pulling out paper plates for the pizza and getting glasses out of the cabinet. Erica concentrated on the child at the table.

Jilly held up the drawing. "See, this is America."

"I see. That's good."

"I can't trace so good with my left hand. Texas looks dumb."

"No, you just need to come down with the tip of it a little farther."

Jilly worked on the adjustment.

"See?" said Erica. "Perfect."

Adam held a plate in his hand and watched Erica leaning over the table, helping his daughter to draw her map. He felt both the protective need to growl at the hovering presence and, at the same time, pleasure in the sound of two soft feminine voices in his kitchen. Beyond both of these, he was aware of a sustained heat pressing through his body. He couldn't stop himself from noticing the way her leather pants hugged her hips, the slick fabric contrasting sharply with the softness of the sweater she wore. He thought about laying his hand against the leather, knowing it would feel cool, then pressing upward slowly until his fingers were warmed by the white wool.

He tore his eyes away, concentrating on the hot pizza in front of him.

"Are we going to eat that or are you just going to stare at it all night?"

He glanced up at Erica, grinning as she spoke, and at Jilly, laughing at him. "You mean I have to share this?" he asked. "I thought this was *my* dinner."

"Daddy," Jilly said with mock exasperation. "We like pizza, too. Don't we, Erica?"

"It's my favorite."

Jilly's eyes widened as she turned an adoring gaze on Erica. "Mine, too!"

Nervous, but realizing things were going pretty well so far, Adam started to relax. "Well, sit down then, ladies." He pulled a chair out for Erica, then hurried around to pull one out for Jilly.

Jilly jumped up from her chair. "You forgot napkins, Daddy." She looked at Erica. "He always forgets something."

"That's men, for you," said Erica.

"Yep," agreed Jilly. "That's men."

Adam smiled and opened the bottle of soda, pouring it into the glasses of ice he had set on the table. He leaned toward Erica. "We have wine, if you'd prefer that."

"No, this is just fine."

Jilly sat back down and started digging into her pizza. "Hurry up so we can decorate the tree."

Erica didn't remember when she had eaten a meal so quickly, but with Jilly hustling everybody along, there was no time for lingering. "Come on, guys. Let's go decorate the tree. A friend gave it to us, you know," she told Erica. "It's real pretty. And tall, too."

Erica shared a secret smile with Adam as they threw away the box and the paper plates and stacked the glasses in the sink. Erica was aware of every infinitesimal space that existed between his arm and hers, his hand and hers, his body and hers.

"Want me to wash them real quickly?" she asked, hoping to insert a modicum of sanity into the evening.

He reached out to stop her hand from turning on the water. "No, I'll get them later."

They both stared at the spot where his hand touched the wool sleeve that covered her arm. She looked up at his face. His eyes, normally as gray as storm clouds, now held a glint of something more urgent. His breath quickened and she felt the rise and fall of her own chest. "No," he said again, this time softly. He slowly pulled his hand from her arm, and she was aware of a keen sense of loss. It deepened when he stepped away.

While the moment had seemed long and suspended, it had actually comprised only the briefest of seconds. Jilly was unaware that anything had transpired in the room around her.

They followed her as she led them into the living room. The room was large and formal and impressively decorated. No expense had been spared. But there was something cold about the room, something lacking life.

The tree sat in the middle of the room, lost and rather forlorn looking in the formal atmosphere.

"We couldn't decide where to put it," said Adam. "We thought about the den, but—well, this is where Marilyn always put it."

Erica could tell he was not comfortable in this room. She wondered if Jilly felt the same. "Where do you want the tree, Jilly?"

Jilly glanced at her father. "Wherever Daddy wants it."

Erica decided somebody around here was going to have to do some prodding. "Can I see the den?"

"Sure," said Jilly, taking Erica's hand. "Come on. I'll show you."

The room she was led into was paneled in a honey-colored wood, and it was filled with older, more worn furniture. It was a well-loved room, with nothing formal about it, nothing untouchable. Erica immediately liked it and felt at home. "This is a great room," she said. "The tree would look perfect in that corner over there."

Adam and Jilly stood undecided, neither saying what they really wanted.

"I like the idea, Daddy," she said hesitantly.

"So do I," he said.

"Well, then," urged Erica.

Adam smiled. "It's perfect. I'll bring it in."

Jilly was about to jump out of her skin, she was so excited. But Erica had noticed before that Jilly rarely let childish glee get the best of her. She was very adultlike. "Let's go get the decorations, Erica."

"Okay, where are they?"

"In the hall. I can drag the little ones, but you'll have to help with the big ones. My right arm doesn't work too good. You probably didn't know that."

Erica did know that, but she wasn't about to say so. "Sure, I'll help. Let's go get them."

While Adam carried the tree into the den and set it in the stand full of water, Erica dragged box after box of baubles and bangles into the room.

Adam laughed at her. "You're not tired, are you?"

"Why am I wasting money on aerobics classes? I should just do this all day."

"Sit down and relax. It's going to take awhile to get these lights on."

Erica sat in a big overstuffed chair and propped her feet on the ottoman.

"That's where Daddy always sits," said Jilly.

Erica ran her hands along the arms and nestled in, smiling up at Adam. "Somehow I knew that."

He turned away quickly and busied himself with the lights while Jilly unwrapped the ornaments. This was too easy. Too natural. It was wrong. He had responsibilities that he mustn't forget. He had made a terrible mistake and, in the process, had lost his wife and the little girl he once had. Being with Erica made him forget all that, and it was wrong. He must not forget. Jilly would never be able to. He didn't deserve to, either. Even for an evening.

And yet . . . he noticed that Erica had kicked off her shoes and pulled one leg up under her. She looked relaxed, at home, very much a part of the room. He wanted to make her a part of him. He wanted to lose himself, just for a little while, in her perfect little world. He craved a respite from his own harsh reality. He wanted softness and tenderness and beauty. Was that so wrong?

Adam was a bundle of raw contradictions. On the one hand, he had never been so uncomfortable in his life. Erica Manning, he knew, had to be bored to death. She was used to fine restaurants, ballets, quiet formal dinners. He also felt as if she were an invader, coming into his home, making judgments, critiquing him and his daughter. He wished she would go. He couldn't stand the way his nerves felt like live wires. She was moving too close to the inner part of him. He could smell her perfume and see her pale hands resting on the armrest where his usually did.

Erica couldn't believe she was sitting here in this comfortable den, decorating a Christmas tree with the two of them. It was just like a real family. It was something she had never done. Her mother had stayed in her bedroom most of the time, lying in bed or propped in a chair with mounds of blankets covering her legs. Her father, she recalled, had closed himself off from his wife in his study, allowing Erica to come in and sit while he worked. She would sit quietly, reading a book, and her father would look up sometimes and beam at her. On the few occasions when she sat in with her mother, her father's face had clouded over with hurt. Erica learned very early whom she must appease in her family.

As soon as the lights were strung around the tree, Jilly starting passing out ornaments for each of them to hang. Most of them were beautiful and expensive, but Jilly had brought in her foil stars and hung them all in the front.

"Save one of those for the top," said Adam. "Or maybe Erica would like one of those for her office door."

"Very funny," Erica said.

"Are you really a movie star?" asked Jilly.

Erica laughed. "Goodness no! Your father was being facetious."

"You were, Daddy?"

"I was teasing her, Jilly."

"Daddy says you're on TV, so you must be a movie star."

Erica glanced at Adam, then back at Jilly. "No, I'm a journalist."

The girl stared with her adultlike expression. "What's that?"

"A journalist is someone who tells what's going on in the world. My job is to interview people, to talk to them about things that are important."

"Like what?"

"Well, like I talked to your father a couple of weeks ago. Did you see him on TV?"

She looked at Adam, and a proud little smile crept over her face. "Yeah. My daddy's handsome, isn't he?"

Adam cleared his throat and looked embarrassed, but Erica grinned at him. "Yes, Jilly, he is."

"Did you have to go to school to be a—a journalist?"

"Yes, I did."

"I bet you didn't have to, though. You're so pretty, I bet they would have wanted you to work for them even if you were dumb."

Erica forced a laugh, unable to push aside the truth inherent in Jilly's remark. She looked at Adam and his eyes narrowed on her, seeing, she suspected, the insecurity she tried so hard to hide.

"Don't you think she's pretty, Daddy? You said so the other night."

Adam kept his eyes trained on Erica. She was nervously fingering an ornament in her hands, and her expression had lost the confidence that most people saw there. She looked very vulnerable right now, and he had the strong urge to take advantage of that vulnerability, to seize the moment and wrap it around him. But they were both waiting for his answer. His eyes remained fixed on Erica as he spoke. "I think she is both very beautiful and very intelligent."

"Me, too," said Jilly, her matter-of-fact tone pulling the two adults out of their trancelike state.

They all stood back and admired the tree. "What do you think, Jilly-girl?" Adam asked, pleased by the light of happiness that had come into his daughter's eyes tonight.

"I love it! Don't you, Erica?"

"It's lovely."

Jilly looked up at her new friend, and her smile was filled with adoration. "I bet your Christmas tree is pretty, too, isn't it, Erica?"

Erica thought of the few decorations she had bought to cover her tree and of the sterile town house in which it sat. She couldn't help but compare her place to Adam's. His house was warm and full of love. Hers was cold and sparse and lonely. "Not as pretty as this one, Jilly."

The little girl walked over to the tree and took off one of her foil stars. She brought it back to Erica. "You can put this on your tree and then it will be as pretty as ours."

Erica felt a lump form in the back of her throat as she gazed down at the child, a child whose life had been so ravaged by tragedy but whose spirit had lost none of its will to live and know joy. By comparison, Erica felt totally inadequate.

She smiled at the child. "Thank you, Jilly. This will go at the top. A place of honor."

## Chapter Ten

While the two adults cleaned up the tissue paper and the boxes that housed the decorations, Jilly crawled up into Adam's big chair with a stack of Christmas books.

Erica set the boxes back in the hall where she had found them. "Do these go in this closet?"

Adam came up behind her with another box. He opened the closet. "Doesn't look like there's any space for them here. Etta got them down from the hiding place." He shrugged. "I really don't know where Marilyn kept them. Crazy, isn't it?"

Erica was watching him closely as he shut the closet door. He kept his hand on the knob and stared at the floor.

"She—she must have been very organized," Erica offered weakly.

He looked back at her. "Yeah, she was."

The self-doubts began to surface once more, and she wondered if he was comparing all the little things about his wife with her. "I'm not the least bit organized," she said, forcing it out into the open.

He turned around and leaned back against the closet door. "Neither am I. Half the time I forget to take something out of the freezer in the morning for dinner at night. I forget things at the grocery store. I don't remember Jilly's appointments. It's so strange. I was always known as a decisive person. If options arose I made a choice. But over the past year, I don't know, I've found it harder and harder to make even the simplest of decisions. I'm fine as long as I'm at work, but the minute I step through this doorway..." He shook his head.

Erica stepped close to him. "That's understandable, Adam. You have a lot on your mind."

"Yeah." He closed his eyes and smiled crookedly. Opening them, he stared at her, then reached out and pulled her up against him. Looking at her soft, upturned face and those blue eyes smiling at him, only one thought now dominated his brain. It surged upward through him, filling his body. The will to resist her was gone. He reached out with his hand and lay it against the side of her neck, drawing her near. His head lowered and he covered her mouth with his own.

Shock waves reverberated through her body when his lips first touched hers. In one smooth motion, he had taken over. His arms closed around her body as his mouth fastened over hers. His hand slid down her back and over her hips. Her pulse began to thunder in her ears and she knew he had to hear it, too. There was an uncontained urgency in his kiss that scared her to death. She didn't want to need this feeling so desperately. It scared her to think that she wanted it to go on and on forever.

It was much too soon when he pulled back and stared down at her with a hopelessly lost look. His chest rose and fell unevenly, and his breath was quick and shallow.

His voice was ragged and strained. "I'm fighting this, Erica. But I'm losing."

She searched for her breath and for a piece of sanity left inside of her. She had trouble finding both. "Maybe it shouldn't be a battle."

He held her head against his chest and the sound of his heartbeat filled her ear. "I keep telling myself that I don't need you in my life. That I can't take any more complications right now."

"Maybe we could just be friends," she whispered, knowing it was a lie even while she said it. "I want to be your friend, Adam. I want to be Jilly's friend, too."

"Why?"

She felt pressure behind her eyes, but she wouldn't let any tears fall against him. She wouldn't. "I've never been a friend, Adam," she said softly, the lump in her throat making it difficult to speak. "I—I've never had a friend, either."

His eyes closed and he held her tighter. "Maybe for your first time around you shouldn't have picked a couple of losers."

She ran her hands up the front of his shirt. "You're not a loser. And neither is Jilly. You know you don't believe that. Jilly is a bright, loving little girl. And you—you're sensitive and—and caring. You're a wonderful father."

"Friends are supposed to be honest, Erica."

"I am being honest."

He was quiet for several long seconds, and she was aware only of his heart beating steadily beneath her ear and his breath falling soft and warm on the top of her scalp. "A wonderful father doesn't kill a child's mother," he finally said, his voice a low, ragged whisper. "He doesn't make it impossible for his little girl to live a normal life."

She pulled her head away and looked up at him, but she kept her hands flattened against his chest. "That accident wasn't your fault, Adam."

Her hands moved down the front of his shirt and back up. He closed his eyes in pleasure, but only for a moment. He covered her hands with his. "I was responsible, Erica. That's what you don't understand. I was the father. I was the one who should have been able to take care of them. I should have been able to make it safe and—and—"

"And perfect?"

He sighed. "Yes."

"You don't believe that, Adam. How can you be responsible for everyone else's life? That doesn't make sense."

He gently set her from him and glanced with surprise across the hall. "Hi, honey," he said. "What have you got in your mouth?"

Erica spun around and saw Jilly sitting cross-legged in the doorway behind them. She was sucking on her thumb and staring at Erica with an impenetrable expression.

She slowly pulled the thumb from her mouth but didn't take her eyes off Erica. "Nothin'."

Erica glanced at Adam, but he was watching Jilly very closely. "It's time for bed, sweetheart."

Jilly didn't move. She still looked at Erica. "Are you going to tuck me in, Erica?"

"If you'd like."

Jilly stood up slowly and walked over to Erica, taking her hand. "I'll show you my room."

"I'd like that very much."

Jilly finally smiled. "Good. Then, come on. You can come, too, Daddy."

She walked Erica up the stairs with Adam following behind. Erica wondered what had been going through the child's head a few minutes ago. Her face had been filled with such sober reflection. But now Jilly acted as if nothing were wrong. She dragged Erica around the room, showing her everything, all of her toys, her books, her clothes.

Adam couldn't remember when he'd seen Jilly so animated. It brought to mind another little girl, the one who used to live here before the accident. It never occurred to him that maybe, just maybe, that same little girl had been here all the time, that he just hadn't been willing to let her reveal herself.

After the fifteen-minute tour of the room, Jilly, wearing an Alf nightshirt, crawled between the sheets of her white wicker bed and adjusted the covers. She lined up her stuffed friends in some kind of preordained pecking order and glanced briefly at the photograph on the table beside the bed.

Erica's gaze lighted on the picture. Inside the frame was a pretty woman with short dark hair, a healthily tanned face, dynamic steel-bright eyes, and a no-nonsense set to her mouth. As much as she hated to admit it, she could plainly see why Adam was reluctant to start a new relationship. He must miss his wife very much.

She felt him behind her, watching her. She turned and forced a smile. What was he thinking? Was he again comparing her to his wife. *Oh, God, what had she gotten herself into!* She had told Adam she wanted to be friends. But she knew, in those rare moments when she was truthful with herself, that she would never be satisfied with that alone. She was very much afraid that she had fallen too much in love with him, with a man who was in agony over his wife's death, with a man who had no room for another woman in his heart.

Jilly had already slid down in the bed, oblivious of the tangled web of turmoil within Erica's mind. "Can you come over tomorrow?"

Deep inside, Erica wanted nothing more than to come, but she knew she had to say no. This was all happening too fast. This need for Adam and his daughter was exploding in a frenzy. It was so complicated! So difficult! She had to think about this, make sense of it, see where they both fit into her life. She didn't want to be simply a replacement for a lost wife and mother. A substitute. Second best.

But she knew that saying she would be having lunch with her father was not a good enough excuse for Jilly so, blurting out the first thing that came to mind, she said, "The television station where I work is having its Christmas party tomorrow. I have to go to that."

"What kind of party?"

"Well, they're—we're taking the Texas Limited to Galveston."

"What's the Texas Limited?"

Adam pulled the covers up over her. "It's a train, Jilly."

The little girl bolted upright. "A train! A real one?"

Adam was surprised by the outburst. She had been subdued for so long, he wasn't yet prepared for the old ebullient Jilly he once knew. "Yes."

Her excited gaze jumped from Erica to her father. "Not like the one at the zoo. You mean a big one?"

Erica's heart began to pound. Something was forming inside of her, an idea. One that she didn't like at all. It kept building, billowing upward, expanding, until without any conscious thought, it exploded from her throat. "Would you like to go, Jilly?"

Adam spun around and stared at her, stupefied. "No!" he said sharply.

Erica herself was stunned. What was she thinking? She couldn't take Jilly to the company party. That was inconceivable.

Why not? her inner voice demanded. Why the hell not? Because it wouldn't work. These were people she worked with. It wouldn't be fair to...to Jilly, of course. Her panicked gaze locked with Adam's stony glare. Disgust for herself and her thoughts mingled with the panic. Her concern wasn't for Jilly and she knew it. It was for herself. *Admit it, Erica. You're afraid to face the world with that little girl by your side.*

Pressure built behind her eyes as she watched the child's face subside from utter ecstasy and childlike glee to its habitual mask of adultlike acceptance.

Erica wanted the joy back. She wanted to make Jilly smile once again. She looked at Adam and lifted her chin. "I'd like for you and Jilly to go with me."

He shook his head.

"It's the 'Dickens on the Strand' festival," she added. "Christmas."

"She has therapy tomorrow." Adam glanced down at Jilly. "You have therapy, Jilly." Her face was grave, her fist clenched around the cover, waiting expectantly but with a painful certainty of what his answer would be. He couldn't do it. He couldn't let her be exposed to those people. Journalists. Snoops. People who made their living out of exposing the suffering of others. He wanted to tell her absolutely not, but his daughter's eyes wouldn't let him escape where he wanted to go, where he knew he needed to retreat for safety.

"Please," Erica heard herself say again, although she wondered if she was pleading with him to say no. Fear coiled through her at the thought of how her life would change if he said yes. No longer would people see her in the same way. No longer could she stay immune. *Please, Adam, please say no.*

"Jilly," he said in a voice that was barely above a croak. "Are you sure, honey?"

"I want to go, Daddy. I want to go with you and Erica on a real train."

He lay her back down in the bed and pulled the covers up once more. His mouth was a grim straight line. "Then we will go," he whispered.

"You'll call Dr. Rhodes and tell him I can't come tomorrow?"

"I'll tell him."

"I love you, Daddy."

Adam's voice faltered. He cleared his throat but was unable to answer her. He stood up straight, and Erica saw the tears glistening in his eyes. Without looking at either of them, he walked out of the room and into the hall.

Now that she knew there was no escape from whatever might happen tomorrow, a sweet pain, unlike any she had ever known, filled Erica's chest. She looked down at the little girl and smiled. "I'm glad you're going with me."

"Me, too."

"Good night, Jilly."

"Night, Erica."

Erica walked to the door and flipped off the light. Adam was standing at the far end of the hall, his hand flattened against the wall, his head hanging down.

"Erica?" Jilly called out before she left.

Erica stuck her head back in the doorway. "Yes?"

"Will you leave the hall light on for my daddy? Sometimes he gets scared."

Erica looked at the little girl and then down the hallway at the man who had turned around and was staring at her with a bleakness that sent a sharp pain to the center of her soul. And she knew, in that moment, that she had been wrong when she thought she could come into this family's life and then walk back out at any time. She was caught firmly in some unseen grasp. And there probably was no escape. She was falling hard and fast, and she wondered if there would be anyone this time to cushion her fall.

"Yes, sweetheart," she heard herself say in a voice that seemed to come from a great distance away. "Yes, I'll leave the light on for him."

She walked slowly down the hallway toward him, the two of them watching each other intently, as if for road signs that might point the way. She was taking a detour in her life, she knew that. One she had not anticipated. The road less traveled by, the Jeep trail through the wilderness. Would she be able to find her way back to her old route? Or would she be lost forever, wandering the hillsides, searching for answers?

She stopped in front of him, her face tilting upward, and she saw the confusion and anxiety that he was trying to keep hidden.

"She's going to be fine, Adam. I promise."

He leaned back against the wall and let out a slow breath. "What if someone says something? Points at her."

"I won't let them. I won't let anyone hurt her. Or you, Adam."

The palm of his right hand remained flattened against the wall. His other hand went to her arm, his fingers spreading slightly over the sweater, devastating her with this simple touch.

He leaned down slowly and touched her lips with his, a tentative kiss this time, testing the depth, surprising her with his gentleness.

Her eyes closed, and her head fell back into the mold of his hand. His mouth trailed to her temple and then to her ear, slow kisses that carefully disguised the barely restrained needs inside him.

She stared at him, unable to move. She couldn't find her breath. She wanted him, had thought night after night of him, of a moment like this where he might lay his fingers on her body. She had thought of the passion that must be bottled up inside him. She wanted desperately to be the receptacle of that passion, but she was scared of what she would be asked in return.

Hot tears pooled in her lower lids and spilled over, running in warm rivulets down her cheek. His fingers gently wiped away the moisture. Her cheek lay flat against his palm, and his thumb stroked over her parted lips. His eyes were still moist and glazed with a need that went beyond physical, a need that scared and exhilarated her at the same time.

Her hands lifted to each side of his face. She tried to smile, but her lips were quivering from emotions that were too difficult to define. "Adam," she began, wanting to explain to him that she wasn't about to be his wife's substitute, that if that was what he was looking for, she just couldn't . . . wouldn't . . .

His mouth came down over hers, sweeping her up into a place she longed to be, into a vast field of forgotten dreams and hopes. Her arms closed around his neck, and his hands looped around her back, fanning out over her hips, one flattened palm pressing against her spine as it slid upward to the back of her head.

"We can't stay here in the hall," he whispered against her mouth.

She felt the pounding of his heart, matching the rhythm of her own.

"Yes. Jilly," Erica murmured against the roughened skin of his cheek.

"Yes." He held her close for a long second and then released her. Taking her hand, he led her across the hall, into another bedroom and closed the door.

The room was dark and warm, and when he wrapped his arms around her once more, she fell into the depths of all that he was offering her.

Now his breath was uneven and ragged and his hand moved down her neck, sliding over the front of her sweater. "You feel so good. I can't believe you're here with me."

Her eyes closed as his fingers stroked over her breast. She felt the sweater glide up over her bare skin. "I'm here."

"Good," he whispered, and his hands began an urgent exploration against her exposed skin. His lips moved like the sea over her throat and onto her shoulder, and his hands moved down the slick fabric that covered her hips and legs.

With one large hand, he pulled her up into the juncture of his body. He had thought of this moment. He had dreamed it, and the dream had washed away the fears and the pain and the loneliness. He couldn't let her go. He needed the dream to be real. Just for a little while. Just for the night.

Lifting her in his arms, he carried her to the bed and came down over her, fully clothed, moving against her, prolonging the sweet agony. "This is where I've dreamed about you, Erica."

With her arms looped around his neck, she pressed up against him, sharp arrows of heat catapulting through her at the places where their bodies met. "I'm not a dream, Adam. I'm real."

They reached for each other blindly, feverishly, fusing all the pain and loneliness into a sweetness they could taste and smell and wrap around them, losing themselves completely, falling into the place where dreams and reality became one.

THROUGH THE WINDOW she could see the Christmas lights on the neighbor's house. She ran her hands slowly up Adam's bare chest. "Do you have lights for the outside of your house?"

His fingers threaded slowly through her hair. "I suppose. Somewhere."

"Your house would be beautiful with lights on it."

Grasping her under the arms, he pulled her up over him. "Are you trying to get me in the holiday mood again, or something?"

She kissed his neck and ran her mouth up along his chin. Her hips pressed into him. "Something like that."

His breathing accelerated. "It's working."

She brushed her lips over his. "It's my new tactic."

"Decking-the-halls seduction scene. I like it."

She lifted her head to look down into his eyes. The light from the hall slipped under the door, throwing his face into planes of shadow and light. "I like you, Adam Bech."

He studied her for a long serious moment. "I like you, too, Erica Manning."

"Does this mean we're friends?"

His hand ran down her back and over her hips. "Something like that."

"Good friends?"

He rolled her beneath him and lowered his head. "The best," he breathed onto her parted lips.

## Chapter Eleven

The drive to the train station was tense and quiet. Erica had left Adam's bed and his house before dawn. Neither of them had wasted the time with sleep.

Later that day, when Jilly and Adam came to her apartment to pick her up, Jilly stayed between them, blocking any encouraging words that might have eased the moment between the two adults. Erica was going to have to be with him all day, close enough to touch him but unable to do so. What was he thinking? Did he regret the night and what they had shared between them? Did he feel that he had betrayed his wife? Did he wish it had never happened? She wished, just once, that the veil would lift from his eyes so that she would know what he was thinking.

Adam gripped the steering wheel and stared straight ahead. He was a mass of exposed nerves, like an animal that had been run over and lay open and bleeding. He had wanted Erica Manning in a way he had thought impossible. But he had thought that once it was over, that once he had vanquished the starving animal inside of him, the driving need would go away. He was wrong. Watching her leave his house had been painful enough. But now, seeing her in a pale yellow sweater and gray slacks, her blue eyes reflecting all the emotion he too felt, he wanted her again. He didn't know how he was going to be with her all day and not touch her, not sink himself into her love once more.

As they drove the freeway toward downtown, Erica made idle chatter with Jilly, who was sitting between them in the front seat.

Jilly was wearing a jeans jumper with a pink-and-yellow checked shirt beneath it. Erica marveled at how well Adam did with her. He always had her dressed so nicely, and her hair was brushed and held back on the sides with two big barrettes. She suddenly realized that it would be nice, very nice to be able to take care of a little girl like Jilly, to help her dress, to fix her hair.

"Is it a big train, Erica?"

"Well, it is five cars."

"Is that big?"

"Not too big. But it's very nice. All the cars have been redone and are beautifully decorated."

"You mean you've been on it before?"

"Yes. I got to go on its maiden run."

"What do you mean?"

"Its first run to Galveston. They stopped running trains to Galveston twenty years ago. They started them up again recently."

"That's neat. Are you excited, Daddy?"

Adam glanced down at Jilly and tried to smile. "Sure, honey. Are you?"

"I can't wait!"

They arrived at the Amtrak station on Washington Avenue only fifteen minutes before the scheduled departure. Erica wondered if the reason Adam had been so late to pick her up was because he really hoped they'd miss the train.

They walked through the station, Adam holding tightly to Jilly's hand. Erica stayed just behind them, her stomach tied up in knots, worrying, wondering if she had made a big mistake in bringing her here.

And then she saw Jilly's face. Her eyes were as bright as twin beacons as she looked at the shiny train up ahead of them.

Erica looked at Adam's face and saw no such excitement. His mouth was drawn into a tight worried line, and his eyes shifted from side to side.

"There's Larry," Erica said, pointing down the tracks. She had the tickets in her hand. "We're supposed to be on the Silver Queen car." She waved to Larry and he smiled and waved back. Several of her co-workers turned to stare as she walked down the dock. She wondered if they were staring because she never attended company functions or because of Adam Bech beside her... or because of Jilly.

*Well,* she thought. *Here goes nothing.* She smiled with encouragement at Adam, and looping her arm through his, they walked toward the group of her co-workers who were waiting to board the train.

She introduced Adam and Jilly to everyone, trying to harden herself against the sometimes curious, sometimes pitying stares. She found herself glaring at anyone who dared to gawk at Jilly like that. She glanced down at the child, but Jilly's attention was on the train, and she was shifting impatiently from one foot to the other, eager to board.

Erica tried to focus on the train, as well. "It is pretty, isn't it?" she said to Adam.

He looked at her, panic-stricken, but he tried hard to find some enthusiasm. "Yeah. It's nice."

Her hand slid down his arm, and she entwined her fingers with his, squeezing gently. "It's going to be fun for her, Adam."

His hand gripped hers tightly, as if he were hanging on for dear life. He tried to smile. "God, I hope so!"

He was sorry when she let go of his hand to move forward with the crowd. He was counting on her, depending on her to help him through this. She seemed so confident that it would all work out okay. He wished he felt the same. From the minute he picked her up at her place, she and Jilly had been chattering and laughing and carrying on as if nothing was about to happen. Why couldn't Erica see the risk they were taking?

He glanced over at her. He had trouble believing that they had actually been together last night. In his bed. Making love. Just the thought of her in his arms was enough to make his blood boil once again. He hadn't wanted her to leave this morning. He had tried to make her stay. But she'd had the good sense that he couldn't find. She knew what the consequences would be if Jilly woke up and saw her there.

They boarded the train. Adam and Erica sat across from Jilly on the pale-green-and-white couches. The train had been refurbished with a local businessman's dream to reinstate rail service between Houston and Galveston. The car they were in had been beautifully restored, with red curtains, pale-green-and-white couches, and Victorian lighting. The bar and all the window trim were made of mahogany.

A white-jacketed waiter came by collecting drink orders and told them that the Silver Queen had been named after an Aspen mine that had produced the largest single silver nugget ever discovered.

The noise from the station crowd was raucous and lively. Champagne flowed freely, and everyone nibbled on little roast beef sandwiches and large boiled shrimp. Even Adam relaxed and began to enjoy himself.

As the train rolled out of the station and south along the tracks toward Galveston, Jilly occasionally waved to motorists on the highway. They passed through Pasadena, Webster, Dickinson, and La Marque. At each town, people waved wildly, happy to see the historic cars rocking through their towns once again.

Adam leaned over and laid his hand on her denim-covered knee. "What do you think, Jilly-girl?"

She had been staring out the window at the blur of passing scenery for the past fifteen minutes. She turned to her father with a huge grin. "It's neat, Daddy! I wished we lived on this train."

To see that smile on his little girl's face, a smile that spoke of happiness and the absolute thrill of living, made all of his own pain and doubts worth it. It had been too long. They had been living in darkness for so long, he had almost forgotten how to find the light.

Erica had brought it back into their lives.

The producer of Erica's show came by and was introduced to Adam and Jilly. Adept at handling any kind of awkward situation, the man was pleasant and easygoing.

"Uh-oh," she said when the producer left. "I can see Larry's had too much to drink."

"What's he going to do?" Adam asked.

Erica shook her head, worried. "Who knows."

Larry came over and sat down on the coffee table. He reintroduced himself to Adam and then grinned at Erica. "How's my gorgeous lady?"

Erica's lips thinned. "Fine, Larry."

He looked at Adam. "Have you ever seen a more perfect face?"

She paled, knowing that he was going to embarrass her in some way. "Larry—"

"I mean she's luscious, isn't she! Gorgeous. The absolute picture of perfection!"

Someone across the aisle murmured loud enough for her to hear, "Yeah, perfect if you've never heard of ethnic groups."

Everyone laughed. Adam reached over and took Erica's hand. "That may be true," said Larry, leaning toward Erica, slightly slurring his words. "But our viewers seem to want that Southern peaches-and-cream look. Right, doll?"

She glanced at Adam. He gripped her hand more tightly and then glanced at Jilly, gauging her reaction to the conversation around her. Larry's back was to the child, as if she didn't even exist.

Erica's face hardened at the patronizing tone Larry was using toward her. She didn't want to be the center of attention, not like this, and especially not with Jilly around. "I don't think this is the place for—"

"And what delivery," Larry cried, slapping his hand against his heart. He growled. "This woman makes me hungry."

Adam stretched his arm over the back of the couch and wrapped it around Erica's shoulder. He stared hard at Larry.

Manda Clark strolled past, a drink in her hand, a smug look on her face. "The question is," she said, loud enough for everyone to hear, "does she understand any of the issues she discusses on the program?"

Larry stood up and weaved slightly in the aisle. "Who the hell cares!" He leaned down to run the back of his hand down Erica's cheek. "See you later, doll."

When he was gone, Erica sat rigid as a chunk of ice, staring out the window. Adam could feel the tension in her shoulders and back, and he wanted to run his hands up and down her spine to make her relax against him.

He leaned close and said, "Hey, don't—"

Erica pushed off the seat. "I'm going to get a drink." Without looking at either of them, she pushed her way down the crowded aisle past the long mahogany bar at the end of the car. Opening the door, she stepped out onto the coupling.

She took several deep breaths of air, trying to still the racing of her heart. Why did Larry have to be such a jerk? When would the competitions ever end?

She stared out over the rice fields that glided past. She had been so happy last night with Adam and Jilly. She had felt so secure and loved. But here, with these people, was where her father thought she should be. This was what she had striven for all her life. She couldn't believe that this was the goal. Not this. Not people like Larry and Manda. Not when there was a bundle of goodness like Jilly and Adam Bech. She realized now that it was her goals that had been distorted. She had never realized, until today, what was really important in her life.

Back on the couch, Adam leaned toward Jilly. "Will you be okay for a minute?"

"Is Erica upset?"

"I think so, honey."

"Did that man say something to make her feel bad?"

"Yes."

"He told her she was perfect. Why does that make her feel bad?"

Adam laid his hand over Jilly's. "I think Erica wants people to see who she is inside and not just what she looks like on the outside."

Jilly glanced out the window, then looked back at her father. "Dr. Rhodes says people always look at the outside first."

Adam felt a lump in the back of his throat, but he nodded.

"Dr. Rhodes says it's hard to make people see who you are on the inside. I think Erica did it real good, Daddy. I like her insides."

The lump filled his chest. "I'll tell her that, Jilly."

When she turned back to the window, Adam stood and made his way down the aisle. Erica wasn't at the bar, but he saw her through the glass door, standing between the cars, the wind whipping her hair. She was so beautiful. He couldn't believe that last night she was really his. He had held her in his arms and they had made love. It was love; he had to admit that. It was not something he had wanted to happen to him. He certainly hadn't planned on falling in love. But despite all the warnings he gave himself, he had fallen anyway. He only hoped that he wasn't setting up himself and his daughter for more hurt.

He opened the door and a blast of warm air hit him in the face. He stepped out onto the coupling beside her, but she kept her gaze directed over the passing land. The railroad paralleled the highway, and motorists rolled down their windows and waved to the rapidly moving train.

Standing behind her, he wrapped his arms around her and kissed her neck, hoping to elicit that beautiful smile of hers.

Leaning back against his chest, Erica said, "Well, now you know."

"Know what?" he asked against her neck.

"How I'm thought of at work. How people see me."

"They're idiots."

"Maybe. Maybe not. I grew up thinking that looks were all that counted, all that mattered. That's the way I've lived my life. Why should people see me any differently?" She turned around in his arms and laid her hands flat against his chest. "Tell me honestly, wasn't it my looks that attracted you to me?"

He swallowed the desire to show her how attractive she was to him, how just looking at her made him grow hot and hungry. He didn't do that, because she needed something more. The problem was he didn't know if he had enough of what she really needed. He had destroyed three lives already. He didn't want to take the chance of destroying another. Still, she waited for his answer. An honest answer.

He smiled. "Yeah, I liked the way you looked." He shrugged. "It helps. I'm sorry. Call me a terrible person, but I couldn't stop thinking about the way you looked."

"But you didn't like *me*."

He sighed and looked out over the ribbon of highway alongside them. The train rocked and jolted, and he grabbed onto the iron railing for balance. "I don't think I've liked anyone much in the last year, Erica."

She observed him closely, looking for signs of lies, signs of truth, searching for all the pieces to Adam

Bech. The wind tousled his hair and ruffled his shirt. She remembered every touch that was shared last night between them. Her fingers sifting through the dark strands of his hair. His mouth, hot and ravenous against hers. His hands everywhere.

But there was so much more to this than the physical. It would be easier if there was not. Being with Adam meant an incredible emotional investment. It meant commitment to a child, a child whose needs went far beyond those of normal children. The thought of such a commitment was frightening, but for the first time in her life, Erica wanted to go inside another person and really know him, really understand what made him tick. He was such a complicated man, and she wondered if he would ever let her come completely inside his world. It was possible that she wouldn't like what she saw and wouldn't want to stay. But she knew she had to see what was there. If she could understand him, maybe she could understand herself.

He had loosened his hold on her so she leaned back against the railing, holding on with one hand. "You know, Adam, I never really cared if anyone liked me before. I always felt that if someone liked me, there was an ulterior motive involved. But with you—I really want you to like me." When he started to speak, she rushed on. "I mean, I know we have something between us. After last night, that's obvious." She laid her hand against his arm, feeling suddenly shy. "It was a wonderful night, Adam. You made me feel things that—"

He grasped her arm and pulled her close, and his voice was husky with renewed desire. "I didn't think I'd ever feel that way again, Erica."

She leaned against him and sighed. "There's more that I need though, Adam. There's more that you need, too. I meant it when I said that I want you to like me. I want to know if there is anything *to* like."

He wanted to tell her there was so much to like. He wanted to tell her all the things that would make her feel good about herself. But the world and all its components had been dark for so long now that he couldn't remember the encouraging words to use. He knew only that he wanted to learn them again, not for himself, but for Erica. And for Jilly.

He held on to her, while the train rocked and creaked and its wheels clacked against the metal track.

Standing in his arms, Erica felt awash with contentment, a sense of belonging to someone, of having someone there to smooth out the rough spots. She closed her eyes and sank into the moment, letting it close around her and fill her.

His chin rested on top of her head, and he was warmed by the feel of her in his arms. But the worries and the doubts wouldn't leave him alone. He had to have answers. "Why did you ask Jilly to come today? You weren't really planning to come to this thing, were you?"

Erica hesitated, knowing that she had to be honest with Adam, but afraid of it all the same. "I don't socialize with these people all that much. I'm sure you can see for yourself why."

Adam stared over her head, wondering where the truth would lead the three of them. "But you said— last night, you said you were coming. You told Jilly that's why you couldn't come to the house."

Erica's heart began a rapid thud inside her chest. She remained still and silent.

"You weren't planning on coming at all, were you?"

She slowly shook her head and it rubbed against his chest.

"You were looking for an excuse?"

She nodded.

He finally released her and, with his hands on her arms, turned her to face him. "But then you asked Jilly to come. Why?"

Erica's eyes closed briefly. The wind felt so good. She wanted it to blow away everything but the pure sensation of being with Adam. "I wish I knew, Adam. I'm so confused about so many things. I like Jilly so much. I'm beginning to care—maybe too much. It scares me."

"Jilly scares you," he said in a matter-of-fact tone, refusing to show any emotional reaction.

Erica knew that this was one of Adam's tests. She didn't know how to pass or fail. She knew only that, for once in her life, she had to be honest with him and with herself.

"I always thought I knew what was important in life, Adam. My father taught me at a very young age that there were only winners and losers. There was health and infirmity. There was beauty and ugliness. Good and bad. Right and wrong. I've lived my whole life in a black-and-white world . . . with nothing in between."

His mouth thinned. "So, in other words, you live in a white world and Jilly and I live in a black one."

"That's what I used to think, Adam. But ever since I met you and Jilly—I don't know, everything is soupy, mixed-up, a gray wash. It's like my whole concept of the world has changed. And that scares me."

His eyes scanned the horizon to the west, and an aching sadness seemed to wash into his voice. "I know what you mean."

Sighing heavily, Erica said, "Do you think Jilly's been alone too long?"

"Yeah. I'd better get back to her."

"I'll come, too."

He smiled at her. "Okay."

He reached to open the car door, but the tone in her voice stopped him.

"Adam?"

He turned and stared at her face, waiting in fear and anticipation for her to say that they had made a mistake. "Yes?" he barely managed.

"Whatever happens between us—wherever this relationship goes...I just want you to know that I think Jilly is perfect just the way she is. I've never known anyone with as much courage and love for life. You've raised a wonderful daughter, and you should be very proud of her and of yourself."

His throat was too tight to speak, but he smiled at her and knew, inside, that if their relationship didn't work, he was going to be a much lonelier man than he ever was.

They made their way back down the crowded aisle. Jilly was absorbed with the passing scenery, but she smiled when they sat back down.

"Sorry we were gone so long," said Erica.

"That's okay. That man came and talked to me."

"What man?" Adam asked, all at once wary.

"That one that was talking to Erica awhile ago. The one who made her feel bad."

"Larry?" Erica asked, stunned. She glanced at Adam and he looked at her, both worried and wondering what careless remarks he might have made to her.

The lines around Adam's mouth tightened. "What did he say?"

Jilly looked at her dad, then at Erica, and then back to her dad. "He said he wanted me to be on TV."

Erica's breath left her lungs in a loud whoosh. "Adam, I swear, I had nothing to do with—"

"On Erica's program?" Adam asked, not even looking at Erica.

Jilly frowned in worry. "I don't have to do it, Daddy, if you don't want me to."

Erica leaned forward and laid a hand on Jilly's leg. "Exactly what did he want you to do, honey?"

"He said you were going to take the TV cameras and stuff to St. Joan's Children's Hospital for a Christmas show."

Adam turned to Erica, glaring at her as if she had planned this whole thing. "And you were going to try to get Jilly on this program?"

"No, Adam! I swear I had nothing to do with this. Look, every year the station tapes a Christmas program at the children's hospital. This year I'm doing it. But I never thought about asking Jilly." She glanced down the aisle and stood up. "I'm going to talk to Larry." She stopped and looked down at Jilly. "I'm sorry, honey. I hope he didn't upset you."

"He didn't upset me, Erica. I want to go."

Erica stared at her for a long moment, then looked at Adam. He was staring at Jilly, too, his forehead drawn.

Erica sat back down. "What do you mean?"

"I mean I want to help you with your Christmas program. Larry said I could maybe help some of those other sick kids."

Adam started to rise. "That son of a—"

Erica laid her hand on Adam's arm. "Adam, wait."

Reluctantly he sat back down. They both watched Jilly closely.

"That's the hospital I was in, Daddy."

"Yes, but you don't have to go back there."

"I might sometime. The doctor says I have to have more operations."

"But not right now, darling."

"I know. But there was a boy like me in the hospital, 'member? And he talked to me and made me feel better. 'Member?"

Adam's hands clenched together, and he had to fight to hold back the pain of remembering. "I remember," he said, his voice a dry croak.

Jilly sat up straight in her seat, looked directly at her father and said proudly, "That's what I'm gonna do."

## Chapter Twelve

When the train crossed the railroad bridge that paralleled the interstate causeway to Galveston Island, Adam's chest grew constricted. The water was calm, but his brain churned like an angry sea.

He used to love the water, used to find it a source of peace. But no more. He hadn't even come back to the Gulf since the accident last year. What was left of the boat was sold for scrap. He'd let the lease run out on his dock. His membership at the yacht club had expired and he hadn't renewed it. The open expanse of the sea held no lure for him now. It represented only one thing—death and destruction.

After a two-and-a-half-hour ride, the train finally made its way into the station at the Galveston Railroad Museum. Stepping off the train was like stepping back in time. Founded first by Cabeza de Vaca, Galveston later became the headquarters for the shady operations of Jean Lafitte. And when Jilly heard the legend that Lafitte's pirate treasures may still lie buried in the shifting sands, her eyes glowed with delight.

They took the trolley from the station to the Strand district, where ten blocks had been turned into a recreation of Charles Dickens's London. The sounds of

Christmas were everywhere; musicians performed on bagpipes, trumpets, violins, dulcimers, tambourines and harpsichords. Victorian carols were sung by a boy's choir.

While the holiday revelers from the television station went off to partake of whatever spirits they could find, Erica, Adam, and Jilly bought hot chestnuts and strolled down the streets, enjoying just being together. The holiday mood was everywhere and, for the first time, Erica felt that it really was Christmas. And Jilly couldn't take it all in fast enough.

"Look, Jilly," Erica called. "There's Tiny Tim. Do you know the story of *A Christmas Carol*?"

"I saw the cartoon on TV."

Adam and Erica laughed. "Do you remember something that we used to call books?" Adam asked with a smile.

Erica was amazed at how well the day was going. Jilly was having a great time, and, though he had gone through some moody moments, Adam was now relaxed. As for herself, she had never felt better in her life. Yes, people stared at the little girl. And yes, people looked as if they were comparing her with the child. But something had happened to her today. Something she couldn't define. It was as if all that she had always been had suddenly vanished. She wasn't a face and a body. She was a person. She felt like one of fifty thousand other people, and it felt great.

Jilly was enthralled by the actors dressed in costume, parading the streets and speaking in Old English. A beefeater of the Royal Palace Guard hurried down the sidewalk after a beggar who was stumping for spare change along the street. And Jilly seemed most excited of all when Adam gave her some money to put into a Salvation Army bucket on the street corner.

Adam felt the tension slide from his shoulders. Jilly was laughing again. He found himself for long minutes forgetting the pain. He even felt the slightest stirrings of the Christmas spirit within him, something he thought he'd never feel again. He looped his arm around Erica's waist and pulled her close, knowing that what he felt today was because of her.

They ate lunch at the Wentletrap and then afterward browsed in antique shops housed in the nineteenth-century iron-fronted buildings.

"I'm getting hungry," said Jilly.

"We just ate a little over an hour ago," her father said.

"I know. But it seems like forever ago."

Erica pointed to an outdoor café across the street. "How about a plum pudding, Jilly?"

"What's a plum pudding?"

"I don't know, but they advertise it, so let's go see what it tastes like."

"Okay." She transferred her hand from Adam's to Erica's, a transference that felt natural and right to both adults.

"While you two girls do that, I'm going to go down to this smoke shop and see if I can find a box of cigars for Dub." He leaned down and kissed Erica lightly on the lips.

A jolt of electricity shot through her at the touch of his mouth on hers, but, at the same time, she felt as if it were the most natural thing in the world for him to have done it.

Adam stepped back, surprised by the fact that he had kissed her so naturally and in front of Jilly. But it felt good. And very right.

When they were seated at the café and Adam had gone, Erica ordered two plum puddings. She enjoyed hers, but Jilly wasn't as enthusiastic about it.

"Don't like it?"

"It's okay."

Erica became aware of a couple of young boys snickering at a nearby table. She glanced over and saw that they were looking at Jilly. She glowered back at them, wondering if she should get up and go tell their parents to teach them some manners.

When Jilly saw what Erica was looking at, she said in a much too adultlike voice, "It's okay, Erica. People think I'm weird."

Erica's chest tightened and she felt pain behind her temples. She wanted to reach out and enfold Jilly, hold her in her arms and make her feel beautiful. It was that dry acceptance, that matter-of-fact tone that hurt the most. She was just a little girl. She should feel that the world was beautiful and good. But at her tender age Jilly already knew that it wasn't always fair. And, unlike Erica and Adam, Jilly could accept that.

"It bothers my daddy more than me," she said, toying with her snack. "He gets real sad sometimes. Real mad, too."

"He loves you very much," said Erica. "That's why he feels sad."

Jilly said nothing, just kept playing with her pudding.

"You know that, don't you, Jilly? You know how much he loves you?"

"I guess."

Erica frowned, wishing she knew how to talk to kids better. Wishing she knew what was going on in their heads. Especially in this little girl's head.

"Dr. Rhodes says Daddy loves me, too."

Erica tilted her head and watched the child. "And you know it's true, don't you?"

"Dr. Rhodes says that when Daddy's scared and sad, that I can help him feel better. Sometimes I don't do it very well."

Erica felt the weight of her own childhood crashing in on her. She knew she had been responsible for her father's moods. If she was perfect, if she won a competition, if she earned praise for her beauty, he was happy. If she lost or didn't put forth the effort to win, he was terribly disappointed in her. She hated that kind of responsibility. It just wasn't fair!

"You can't make your dad happy or sad, Jilly. He's got to do that for himself."

"But I want him to love me, Erica."

She reached over and took Jilly's hand, squeezing it. "He *does* love you. He loves you so much. And that love has nothing to do with whether you make him happy or sad." Erica felt tears welling up in her eyes. "You know, Jilly, you and I have a lot in common."

Jilly looked surprised and shook her head.

"It's true," said Erica. "We're very much alike. My mother died when I was fairly young."

"She did?"

"Yes. And I wanted my father to love me so much."

"You're so pretty. I bet he loved you a lot."

Erica wiped away a loose tear. "He loved me because I was pretty. But I wanted him to love me because of who I was inside."

"Etta and Daddy were talking about you. They said you were a beauty queen. I didn't know what that meant, but Etta said you wore a crown and long dresses and everything."

"Yes, I did all that. And, when I was winning these beauty contests, my father loved me."

"Did you ever lose some?"

"Yes."

"And your daddy didn't love you then?"

"I think that, deep down inside, he really did love me, but—well, he wanted—I guess he thought that he could make me what *he* wanted me to be. He wanted this perfect little girl, because it meant he had done something right. Does that make sense?"

Jilly stared at her and Erica knew she was trying hard to understand. She was the type of child who wanted answers. She wanted to know what made the world tick, and she desperately wanted to know what her place was in it.

"Sorta."

"What I'm trying to say is that he wanted to be the perfect father. And, if I was perfect, then he was doing a perfect job. You see what I mean?"

She nodded. "And if you didn't do perfect, he thought he was doing a bad job?"

Erica sighed. "Yes, I think so."

"Does my daddy think he is not doing a good job?"

Another wayward tear fell onto Erica's cheek. "I think so, honey. I think he feels that if nothing had happened to you, if he could have kept you safe, then he would have been a good father. He feels that what happened to you is his fault, and that makes him feel bad about himself."

Jilly sat still for a minute, absorbing all that Erica had said. Finally her mouth turned down and she said, "Poor Daddy."

"Well, I'll tell you what," said Erica, pulling a tissue from her purse and dabbing it beneath her eyes. "We'll work on him together, okay?"

"Okay. How?"

"Well, we'll just hug him and kiss him and take such good care of him, he won't have any room for sad thoughts."

Jilly's eyes widened excitedly. "You think it will work?"

Erica shrugged and smiled. "I don't know, but it's worth a try, don't you think?"

"And can we make his bad dreams go away, too?"

Erica's heart began to race. Commitment time. That was what this was. This was not some whim of the moment. This was major commitment. Did she have it within herself to give that much? Was this what she really wanted in her life? Her eyes were captured by the penetrating stare of the little girl across from her, and she suddenly knew what the answer was.

"Yes, Jilly, we can make those bad dreams go away, too."

Jilly sat back and smiled happily, blindly accepting Erica's assumption that the world would be right once again.

"Look over there!" Jilly cried.

An old man, costumed in pauper's clothes, waved at Jilly from across the street. Jilly stared at him until he stuck out his tongue. Then she giggled and waved back. Erica smiled.

"Those actors are good, aren't they?"

"They look so real," agreed Jilly.

After standing there a minute and making faces at her, the old man crossed the crowded street and came up to the sidewalk table where Erica and Jilly sat. His toothless grin was a wholly believable touch. His shirt was tattered, and the cuffs of his pants were rolled unevenly.

He was looking only at Jilly, as if no one else in the café even existed, and Erica's heart began a rapid beat. There was something about him that both frightened and exhilarated her. She knew Adam wouldn't have encouraged the man at all, but Erica felt that there was something so gentle about him, so right. Despite his haggard, ratty appearance, his eyes glowed like two beacons of light. He smiled crookedly.

He hadn't said anything at all. He was just looking at Jilly and she was looking at him. But then, from behind his back he pulled out a doll and held it out to Jilly. She stared at it in wonder. Erica, too, stared, unable to think of anything to say.

Made of old cloth, with a porcelain head, the doll was as tattered as the man was, with torn clothes, unkempt hair, an eyelid that didn't open properly. One of its porcelain arms was missing.

The man still said nothing, just smiled and held it out to her, nodding his head slowly.

Jilly reached out slowly and hesitantly, wanting to touch the antique doll, but afraid he might not want her to. The man, still not speaking, nodded his head again, encouraging her to take it.

She took it from his hands and pulled it down into her lap. Her eyes were fixed upon it, as if nothing else in the world existed. She ran her fingers through the tangled mass of hair, then touched the spot where the arm was missing. The face was blotched with dark stains, but the one eye that remained open was clear and blue.

Jilly stared, transfixed, and then finally she looked up at Erica. Her voice was filled with wonder. "She looks kind of like me."

Erica swallowed the panic. No! she began to stammer, but Jilly was smiling at the doll. She pulled it to her chest and hugged it tightly.

"Is she really mine, Erica?" she whispered almost reverently. She held it out to her, this new prized possession.

Erica didn't know what to say. At one time the doll had probably been very beautiful and very valuable. Now it was something that someone had donated, no doubt, to the Goodwill and that had been retrieved by this actor who dressed as an old derelict.

She turned to ask the man about the doll, but he was gone.

She swiveled in her chair, looking at the other tables to see where he had gone.

"Can I really keep her?"

"Where on earth did that man go?" asked Erica with a frown. He just disappeared!

"Look, Erica."

Erica followed the line of Jilly's finger. She was pointing down the sidewalk where the old man was walking. After a moment, he rounded the corner and was out of sight . . .

"Well," mused Erica. "If that's not the strangest thing I've ever seen."

"I can keep her, can't I, Erica?"

Erica stared at the bedraggled doll, clutched so tightly in Jilly's arms. "Well—I guess so, honey. But

I don't understand why he just gave it to you like that. He didn't say a word.''

Jilly stared down at the doll and smiled. ''I know why he gave it to me.''

''No, Jilly,'' she began, faltering over the words. ''He didn't mean—''

''He knew I could take care of her,'' said Jilly.

Erica's mouth snapped shut and she stared at her. Jilly hadn't spoken sadly or with any kind of self-pity. Her words had been matter-of-fact, adultlike, totally accepting. She believed she knew why the man had given her the doll, and she accepted the responsibility without question.

Erica had never felt so much love for anyone as she felt right now for this little girl.

After a few minutes, when they saw Adam coming down the sidewalk, Jilly waved excitedly. ''Look, Daddy, look what this old man gave me.'' She held out the doll to him.

Adam took it and began to frown. He flipped open the eye with his fingers, but it didn't stay. He examined the clothes and the missing arm and the stains. ''Who did you say gave this to you?''

''This old man.''

He turned to Erica and the scowl deepened. ''What's the deal?''

''She just told you, Adam. This old man—well, actually some actor dressed as a pauper came over and gave it to her.''

He still held the doll in his hands. ''Why?''

Erica glanced briefly at Jilly, then back at Adam. ''He felt it was—right for her, I guess.''

''What the hell is that supposed to mean?''

"Look, Adam," she said, laying her hand on his tense arm, "Jilly likes the doll. Why don't you sit down and have a cold drink or something."

Adam glared at her. "Don't patronize me, Erica. This is serious."

"Can I have my dolly back, Daddy?"

He looked down at Jilly, then at the doll. He turned back to Erica. "What did the man look like?"

"Really, Adam, I don't think—"

"Just tell me what he looked like, Erica."

She sighed and tried not to let Jilly's bewildered expression fill her with ache. "He wore a tan shirt, torn. And his pants were rolled up at the cuffs. His hair was gray. He had lots of it, real thick around his head. And a kind of stubbly beard. He was also missing some teeth."

"Don't I get to keep the dolly, Daddy?"

He wouldn't look at his daughter. He kept his eyes on Erica. "No."

Erica sighed. "Adam, I—"

His mouth was grim, the lines deepening around it. "You don't get it, do you? It's defective. He gave her a defective doll."

"It's okay, Daddy. I can take care of it."

"It's very old, Adam," Erica said gently, hoping to calmly assuage his anger. "I'm sure he didn't mean anything derogatory about it."

"Oh, I'll just bet he didn't." He turned to Jilly. "Look, honey, I'll buy you a doll, a nice new doll. You don't have to settle for this one."

"But I like it."

"I'll buy you a new one." He looked at Erica. "Which way did he go?"

"Down the street that way."

"I'll be back in a minute," he said, his voice a furious growl. He strode off, the doll gripped ruthlessly in his hand, dangling at his side.

"I don't mind, Daddy," said Jilly, but her voice was too weak and he was already too far away to hear.

Erica smiled reassuringly at her, but Jilly's face had settled into a calm, emotionless facade.

On the train ride back from Galveston, Jilly slept on the seat across from Adam and Erica. Beside her, still in the box, was the expensive new doll that Adam bought for her.

At home in her room, Jilly set the doll in the back corner of a shelf. She didn't pick it up again.


DOWN IN THE DEN, with the tree lights on and a Christmas tape playing, Erica sat on Adam's lap in the big overstuffed chair. They shared a bottle of wine.

"Are you going to let her do the program, Adam?"

He sipped at his drink and spoke in a defeated voice. "Looks to me as if I'm outnumbered."

"But you're not happy about it."

He set down his glass and rested his hand on Erica's thigh. He closed his eyes. "She spent months in that hospital, Erica. You don't understand what that was like."

She ran her fingers through his hair. "So, tell me," she said softly.

"I can't."

"Yes, you can, Adam. You need to talk about this."

"You couldn't relate to it."

"Try me."

He leaned his head back and let out a long, slow breath. "She was covered in bandages. And there were tubes everywhere. They didn't think she would live.

They kept telling me to go home and get some sleep, but I couldn't. I knew that if I left, she'd die."

"So you stayed with her the whole time?"

"As much as the hospital staff would let me. And then there was Marilyn's funeral. I went to that."

She leaned over slightly and kissed his forehead.

"Dub and Mo handled everything. I don't remember much of it. I was like this—this shadowy presence. I was functioning solely on remote. When I think back, it's like everything was dark and fuzzy around the edges. I can't focus on any one day or moment."

He opened his eyes and looked at Erica. Slowly he lifted his hand to her head and pulled her down. His mouth moved over hers slowly and gently. When he let her go, he looked at the tree. "You know, I hadn't wanted Christmas to come. I thought if I ignored it, it would leave us alone." He looked back at Erica and smiled tenderly. "You barged in with it, didn't you? You just couldn't let things be."

She smiled back and shook her head. "Nope. Not when I saw the chance to have the first family-type Christmas ever."

"You really didn't do that when you were growing up?"

She snuggled down against him, resting her head on his shoulder. "You know, I remember when I was— oh, I guess seven or eight, somewhere around Jilly's age. I made a Christmas tree out of construction paper and glued all this glitter on it. I took it into my mother's room where she was in bed and I gave it to her. She stared at it for the longest time and then she started crying. She just cried and sobbed. And it really scared me. I hadn't meant to make her cry. I never made anything like that for her again."

Adam brushed his lips across her forehead. "Why do you think she cried?"

She tilted her head to look up at him. "I think she was happy. I didn't know that then. I just knew it scared me. But now I really know that she was so happy that I had made her something for Christmas, that she cried."

He wrapped his arms around her and pulled her tight. "I guess you've been lonely, too, haven't you, Erica?"

"Until I met you, I didn't think so. But I know now that I've always been lonely. All my life. Until now."

"Jilly and I are a package deal, Erica."

She knew that. To have Adam was to have Jilly. They were part and parcel of each other. A unit. To forge her life with theirs would change everything. Nothing would ever be the same again. She knew all of that, but the question that still lingered in her mind was, could she live with that.

Her silence told him all that he didn't want to hear. If she did not want him now, he knew he would have a hard time fitting the pieces of who he was back together. But he also knew that she had to accept everything about his life for any kind of a relationship to work. He understood the realities all too well. Still he couldn't stop himself from dreaming of the possibilities.

"Will you stay the night?"

Her eyes locked with his, and she knew that, for now, he was offering her a home in his arms. But she also knew that the offer was only temporary. Both of them would eventually have to make a permanent choice.

"Yes, Adam, I'll stay the night."

## Chapter Thirteen

Erica and Jilly stood at the counter in her small kitchen, enveloped in a cloud of flour. "Where did you put the snowman, Jilly?"

"Over here. But I want to do a Santa Claus next."

"Okay, well come over and do this. We're going to run out of time. We have to be at the hospital by eleven o'clock. Your dad is coming for us in an hour."

"Do you think the kids will like my cookies?"

Erica smiled and gave her a big hug. "They'll love them."

"I've got one of my stars to take, too," Jilly said. "I hope they have a big tree to put it on."

"I'm sure they will. Did you see where I put your star?"

Jilly grinned. "Yeah, right on the top of your tree. I like your house, Erica. You said it wasn't nice, but I think it is."

Erica laid the cutout cookies on a tray and slid them into the oven. "I said it wasn't as nice as yours."

"Ours is too big." She paused and stared at the cookie cutter in her hand. "It didn't used to seem too big."

Erica reached for a sponge to clean up the counter, trying not to think of how Adam's house must have been when Marilyn was alive. There must have been so much laughter and fun, then. Without his wife, could there ever be again?

"You're fun, Erica," Jilly said, as if she had been reading her thoughts. "This is like being best friends. Can we do this for Valentine's Day, too?"

Erica smiled at her new best friend, hoping that she had the inner strength to make it, not only to Valentine's Day, but to next Christmas, and the Christmas beyond....

"Absolutely," she said with determination, hoping that the word alone would give her the fortitude to make it a reality.

Adam came in for them about ten-fifteen. The cookies were stacked on plates and covered with plastic wrap. And Jilly had insisted on taping bows to the top of each plate.

"You two look great," said Adam, giving Jilly a quick kiss and Erica a much longer one.

"It must be working, Erica," said Jilly when they were kissing.

"What's that?" asked Adam.

"All the hugs and kisses."

His brows drew together and he looked from one to the other. They were both giggling. "What's that supposed to mean?"

Erica winked at Jilly and pinched the tip of Adam's chin. "That's our secret."

"Girl talk," said Jilly.

"Right," nodded Erica.

In the car driving to the hospital, Adam tried not to let his anxiety show. He still wasn't convinced that having Jilly on this program was such a good idea. And at first, he hadn't even planned on coming to the hospital. He had told himself that he absolutely would not.

And yet he parked in the lot and found himself wending his way through the all too familiar corridors, the smell of disinfectants filling him with dread.

Erica took his hand to ease the tension that he couldn't hide, but all he could manage was a weak attempt at a smile.

They turned a corner and passed through the doorways into a new wing. He was aware of the echo of their feet tapping along the gray speckled linoleum floor. Long tubes of fluorescent lights buzzed above their heads.

He glanced over at Jilly. She hadn't said much of anything. But she was taking in everything they passed. Reaching down for her hand, he gave it a light squeeze. She looked up, unsmiling, and he saw that she was afraid.

He stopped in front of a bank of elevators and stooped down in front of her. "You don't have to do this, Jilly."

Jilly glanced up at Erica.

Erica knelt down beside Adam. "It's okay, Jilly. If you don't want to do this, that's fine. Nobody wants you to do something you're not comfortable with."

"It's just a little scary, that's all."

"I knew this was a mistake," murmured Adam. "Come on, Jilly, let's get you out of here."

A nurse walked out of the elevator, pushing a boy in a wheelchair. His arms were wrapped in gauze bandages. Jilly and the boy appraised each other.

"Are you going to the Christmas party?" Jilly asked him.

"Yeah," said the boy. "Are you?"

Jilly looked up at her dad and then back to the boy. "Yes, I'm going, too."

Adam and Erica exchanged a quick glance.

"Jilly—" Adam started.

She looked up and smiled confidently. "Don't worry, Daddy. I want to go now."

As they all stepped onto the elevator, Jilly asked the boy, "Were you in a fire?"

"Yeah."

"Me, too."

Adam lifted his hand to massage the back of his neck. Erica reached for his free hand and held it tightly.

After leaving the elevator, they rounded another corner and heard the commotion. A lighting technician bumped into Adam, mumbling a vague apology, while he made adjustments with the lights. Camera crews wheeled their tripods into place, and Larry stood in the middle of the room, frantic.

"There you are!" he cried. "God, I thought you'd never get here."

Erica checked her watch. "We've got plenty of time." She laughed. "Stop worrying."

"Stop worrying," he mumbled as he walked off to talk to one of the cameramen. "Stop worrying, the woman says...."

Adam hung back against the far edge of the room, waiting with a growing sense of dread for the program to begin.

He could hear Erica talking to various crew members. She was hidden behind the mass of cameras and wires and lights and crew members. He wondered if Jilly was still scared. He hoped Erica would hold her hand.

Once all the children had been brought into the room and the program was running, Adam edged around the crowd of bystanders, some in their green hospital gowns and robes, others in crisp white uniforms. A huge Christmas tree loomed in one corner of the room. Thirty or forty children, some in robes sitting on the floor, others in wheelchairs, and still a few others in portable beds, all clustered around the tree. A volunteer dressed as Santa Claus stood before them, juggling packages in his arms.

Carefully Adam worked his way to the front of the onlookers. And there he saw them, Erica and Jilly standing side by side, holding hands. He tried to read Jilly's expression, but it was too difficult. Her eyes were often the only signal to her thoughts and, right now, she was just too far away. He had the irrational desire to stand in front of the cameras and block their view of her. They were gawking, filming, staring at her. He wanted to break their lenses, smash their faces. He felt his skin grow hot, and his fists clenched at his sides.

And then he saw Jilly smile. The man dressed as Santa Claus bent down and handed her a package, which she, in turn, handed to one of the children in a wheelchair. Jilly helped the little girl open the gift and a round of excited applause went up when the girl saw the stuffed bear inside the box. She hugged it to her chest.

Adam noticed once again how beautiful Erica looked, wearing a mid-calf-length red knit dress, cinched at the waist with a gold belt. One side of her hair was pulled back with a big red bow. She was gorgeous and totally in her element before the lights and cameras. The desire he felt for her was so intense it was frightening. He was beginning to want her too much. He was beginning to need her in his life too much.

Adam's attention jumped from Jilly to Erica and back to Jilly again. They made a good team, the two of them did. Jilly was a formidable child, much like her mother was. But she also had a sweet vulnerability to her that was very much like Erica Manning. He was mesmerized by the two of them together, smiling at each other, laughing with the children, singing songs. Jilly very ably managed to take the packages from Santa Claus and from under the tree and give them to the children. When they had trouble, she was there to lend a hand. He was surprised, once again, by her animation. She was a tiny flurry of blond smiling glee. And his heart was filled with love for her.

Two weeks ago, this day would have been inconceivable to him. Everyone had tried to tell him—Dub, Etta, other well-meaning friends—that he couldn't hide Jilly away from the world. But he had only done it to protect her. He had thought that was the way to keep her out of harm's way. She had been through so much, he just wanted the pain to end.

But Erica had showed him another way. He and Jilly had come a long way since Erica came into their life. He thought now that he just might be able to find his way out of the long dark night through which he had been crawling for so long.

His eyes met Erica's over the tops of little heads, and they smiled. *Thank you,* he wanted to say. *Thank you for bringing joy back into my daughter's life. And into mine.*

The toys that were being given out, he soon realized, were not new ones. Erica began explaining to the audience that everything had been donated from local organizations and church groups, and had been painstakingly refurbished by caring volunteers.

Adam wondered why the hospital hadn't asked for donations of new toys but, after a few minutes, he realized that the decision had been carefully made. As he watched the children opening the presents, he quickly realized that their joy and sense of wonder was due, in part, to the fact that people had cared enough to give a cherished toy to them.

Flashing through his mind was an image of Jilly, sitting on the train seat, a brand-new doll tucked neatly away in its box, buried under mounds of tissue. The room grew hot and stuffy, and he felt as if the walls were closing in.

He watched as Jilly helped a young girl in a wheelchair pull out an especially used-looking doll, with arms and legs that didn't move properly. The girl hugged the doll tightly, and Jilly's eyes were fastened on her and on her doll.

A jagged knifelike pain sliced through Adam.

The little girl kissed the doll.

Adam felt a blow to his chest.

Jilly stared at the girl.

Adam looked at Erica. She too was staring at Jilly. His heart began to pound erratically. When Erica looked up, he saw that her eyes were filled with tears.

In one stunned moment of revelation, Adam realized what he had done. He closed his eyes to keep the room from spinning out of control.

He turned around and charged out of the room. He had to get some air! He had to think! Another mistake! He had made another terrible mistake!

And this one, like the last, was irrevocable. He had taken away a child's mother. He had taken away any chance at a normal life. And he had taken away a gift.

He could try to locate the actor who had given her the broken doll that day . . . if he had found the old man. He hadn't told Erica or Jilly that he hadn't been able to find the old man to return the doll to him. Instead—God, he couldn't believe he had done it!—instead, he had thrown it into a trash can. By now, it was probably lying at the bottom of a big pile of garbage at the city dump.

Erica had turned her attention back to the party at hand, but her pulse was fluttering erratically in her throat. She wondered if she'd be able to find her voice. She hoped she wasn't going to cry in front of the cameras. Why had she let Adam take that doll away from Jilly? Why had she let him give it back to the old man? She should have said something to stop him. She should have insisted. But she hadn't. She had not wanted to commit herself enough to the two of them to stop the terrible mistake. She had kept her emotional distance in an attempt to protect herself. And she had selfishly deprived this child of something that she desperately needed.

Erica blinked back the tears. And she was supposed to be Jilly's best friend!

AFTER THE TAPING of the show, Jilly and Erica found Adam outside the hospital, leaning against the car. He was smoking a cigarette, something she had never seen him do. His expression, when he looked at Erica, was bleak and drawn.

"Hi, Daddy," Jilly said with a smile. "Did you see me?"

He tried to force a smile. "Yes, honey, I did. You—you were great."

"Thank you."

"I didn't know you smoked," said Erica.

"I don't," he said, shrugging.

She stepped up in front of him and placed her hand on his right shoulder. With her other hand, she pulled the cigarette from his mouth. "Uh-huh, then what's this?"

He tried to smile. "How did that get there?"

She pursed her lips, dropped the cigarette to the parking lot and ground it out with her foot. "Don't you think you've punished yourself enough?"

He leaned back against the car. Jilly had climbed into the car and was pulling Christmas tapes out of the glove box. He looked back at Erica and spoke softly. "Sometimes I think I haven't punished myself nearly enough."

"Maybe we can trace the doll down, Adam."

"No, we can't."

"We could contact the actor's guild."

He shook his head and whispered so Jilly couldn't hear. "I threw the doll away."

Erica stared at him, whispering back, "You didn't give it to the old man?"

"I couldn't find him."

So that was it, then. The doll was gone. She and Adam had missed a chance to do something right for a change. Still, she wasn't going to kick herself over and over for it, and she wasn't going to let him, either. "We'll make it up to her, Adam."

He studied the clear blue of her eyes. "How is it that you always seem to make things better for me?"

She kissed him lightly on the mouth. "It's a gift."

He kissed her back, soundly. "I accept."

A car pulled up and a horn honked. Erica turned around and waved in surprise. "Hey, that's my dad. Maybe we can get him to spring for lunch."

Adam grasped her arm, pulling her back. "Listen, Erica. I think I'd like to spend some time alone with Jilly, if that's okay. You know, take her to lunch or something."

"Sure, Adam. I have a few things I need to discuss with my father, too." She waved again to her father and watched him climb out of the car and start walking toward her. "At least come meet him, okay?"

Even from this distance, she could see the hesitancy in her father's face as he drew nearer.

"Hi, Dad," she said, forcing a cheerfulness she didn't particularly feel. "Come here. I want you to meet Adam Bech. Adam, this is my father, Parker Manning."

The two men gripped hands and nodded politely. From the few things that Erica had told him about her father, Adam didn't have any great desire to meet the man. But, for Erica's sake, he put on a good face.

"I've heard a lot about you, sir," said Adam. "It's a pleasure meeting you."

"And in here is Jilly, Dad."

Jilly climbed out of the car. "Hi!" she said.

Parker turned to the child and his smile was strained. He did not offer his hand to her. "Hello."

He turned back to Adam as quickly as etiquette allowed.

"I thought maybe I'd take my daughter to lunch," Parker said. "You're—you and your daughter—are welcome to join us."

The last person that Adam wanted his daughter with was a man like Parker Manning, so he declined politely. "Thanks anyway, but Jilly and I have a date."

"We do?" she asked, looking surprised.

"Yep."

Jilly looked from Erica to her dad. "Won't Erica get mad?"

Erica laughed. "No, honey. You go spend some time with your dad, and I'll go spend some time with mine."

Jilly thought about it, then nodded and said, "I think that's a good idea."

After saying goodbye and promising to come by to see her later, Erica watched them walk away, holding hands, this man and little girl who had such a hold on her life.

AFTER WAITING FOR thirty minutes in the bar for a table, Erica and her father were finally seated near a window. "Well, no snow for you yet," Parker joked. He perused the wine list and suggested a German Riesling.

"I don't want anything to drink today, Dad. I've got to get back to work."

"Oh, come on, they'll give you the afternoon off to be with your old man."

Erica chuckled. "Yeah, right."

Parker grew serious. "Would you have asked for the afternoon off if Adam Bech had been with you?"

She tilted her head. "Dad, do I detect a note of fatherly jealousy here?"

He rested his elbows on the table and stared at her. "We've discussed this before, Erica. You know where I stand."

Erica stared for a long moment out at the sunlit afternoon. She looked back at her father. "And I want you to know where I stand, Dad."

Parker ordered a glass of wine from the waiter and then frowned at Erica. "What the hell is that supposed to mean?"

"I am talking about a man I care for very much. I—I think I love Adam."

"You've been in love before."

She shook her head and smiled. "Not like this, Dad. The way I feel is very different from anything I've ever felt before. He's—I don't know, Dad. I just know I want to be with him all the time. Share his life."

"We've discussed this, Princess. He's not the one for you."

Erica couldn't believe the dismissive tone she heard in her father's voice. "Says who?"

The waiter set down the glass of wine, and Parker stared at Erica for a long moment. "There's no need to be sarcastic, daughter."

"I'm trying to be truthful, Dad. I'm a grown woman. I can make my own decisions in life."

"Yes, you can," he said, taking an appreciative sip of his wine. "As long as they're the right ones."

She leaned forward, resting her weight on her elbows. "Right or wrong, they have to be mine. You've been making them for me all my life. It's time I did it for myself, even if the path is different from the one you would choose for me."

"But—but you've always known what you wanted, Erica. It's the same thing I've always wanted for you."

"I'm not so sure that's true."

Parker's nostrils flared as he barked his lunch order to the waiter. Erica ordered only a salad. She had suddenly lost her appetite. She had not always agreed with her father, but, until now, she had always assumed that he had her best interests at heart. Now she wasn't so sure.

"I love Adam, Dad. And—well, I'm pretty sure he loves me, too. I mean, there are some complications to work out and all, but—"

"Complications?" Parker snorted. "You've got more than complications, my dear. What you've got is a nightmare on your hands."

Erica's brow knitted.

"Don't frown, dear, you'll make wrinkles."

She took a drink of water to give her the time to still the anger that was starting to build inside of her. She wasn't going to lose her temper and lash out at her father. Not here. But it was going to take every ounce of strength to withstand the diatribe she knew was forthcoming from him.

"I assume," she said carefully, "that you are referring to Adam's daughter, Jilly."

He leaned closer, lowering his voice. "You know damn well what I'm referring to. Have you thought about that kid?"

"Very much."

"Erica, after all I went through with your mother, how could you even consider doing such a thing to yourself?"

She had asked herself the same questions, but, coming from her father, they seemed brutal and insensitive.

"What is it that you think I'm going to do to myself?"

"You're going to ruin your life, that's what. Destroy it. Destroy everything I've ever done for you. All the work and the hopes."

"How is Jilly Bech going to destroy my life?"

"Erica, my God! How can you be so blind! Look at you. You are perfect. People want to look at you. Have you noticed all the people in this restaurant staring at you?"

Erica glanced around, all at once feeling naked and exposed. She didn't want people staring at her. The beauty contests were over. This was a different phase of her life. She no longer wanted center stage.

"What does that have to do with Jilly?"

His tone was thick with disdain. "Think, Erica. If she is with you, people will never look at you the same. You can be enhanced or contaminated by the people you're with."

"Contaminated? You think Jilly will contaminate me?"

"God, you don't understand!" He rubbed his temples. "Maybe I protected you too much from your mother. Maybe that's the problem. Maybe I should have let you spend more time with her and see what it was like being saddled with her."

Erica stared at her father, horrified. "How can you talk like that, Dad? She was your wife! My mother! You married her. You must have loved her once."

"I did love her once!" he growled. "She was so pretty. She was the prettiest girl at the dance the night I met her. I fell head over heels in love with her."

"I see. And when she got sick, you fell out of love with her?"

"She changed."

"How?"

"She wasn't the same person."

"Her looks or her?"

He looked away and took a hefty swig of the wine. "It's one and the same."

Erica stared at him for a disbelieving minute. She couldn't believe all the years she had let this man hold her life in his hands. "It's not the same at all, Dad. I used to think it was. But I know now that's not true. Jilly is a perfect example. She's a very special person, Dad. She's smart, she's kind, she's sweet, she's—I don't know, there is so much to her that I haven't even gotten to know yet. If you got to know her, you'd love her."

"People will be repulsed by her."

Erica pushed away the salad the minute it came. "Then that's their problem."

"It will be yours, too. By association, people will be repulsed by you."

She shrugged. "Let them. I don't care."

He shook his head slowly, staring at her. "I'm not sure I know you anymore."

Erica looked at the man who had been her life and her guide for so many years. That man was gone to her forever, and she didn't even have any tears left to shed. She picked up her glass of water and looked at him over the rim, for the first time seeing him as he really was. "No, Dad," she said slowly and deliberately.

"I'm not sure you ever knew me. I'm not sure I knew myself. Until now."

ADAM ORDERED a chocolate milk shake and a grilled cheese sandwich for Jilly and a chicken sandwich and iced tea for himself.

"How come we're eating out?" Jilly asked. "We never do that."

Adam clasped his hands under his chin and took a deep breath. "Do you like to eat out, sweetie?"

"Yes."

"Then we're going to start doing it more."

Jilly kept her hands in her lap, and looked earnestly at her father. "But you don't like to go out, Daddy."

Adam was grateful for the glass of iced tea that was set down in front of him. It gave him a moment to collect his thoughts. When the waitress was gone, he said, "I've been afraid to go out, Jilly. Did you know that?"

She sucked on the straw in her thick milk shake and nodded.

"You did?"

She nodded. "You thought we'd get hurt again."

"Yes," he said slowly. "I did. But probably not in the way you're thinking."

Jilly wrapped her left hand around the glass and worked on the shake while she watched him with those penetrating eyes that saw so much.

"For a while I was afraid of another accident. Remember, we talked to Dr. Rhodes about that."

"I 'member."

"I was afraid of water and fires and—well, all sorts of scary things. You got over those fears more quickly than I did."

"I'm sorry, Daddy."

He reached over quickly and touched her hand. "No, darling, I'm glad you did. It's just that—well, fathers are supposed to be able to take care of their little girls. I haven't done such a good job at that."

"I think you do real good. Etta helps, too."

"Yes, she does." He sighed. "I don't know what we would have done without Etta."

He ran his finger along the back of her hand. "I wanted to take care of you, Jilly-girl, but after the accident, I felt that I had done this terrible thing to you. I kept thinking that I could have done something to stop the accident."

"It wasn't your fault, Daddy."

"I know that, but—" He cleared his throat to try to dislodge the painful knot. He felt something hot and liquid behind his eyes. "I wanted to make your life perfect for you. I wanted—so much."

Jilly pulled her hand back to her lap and stared at the table. Adam watched her, wishing she would tell him what she really thought, wishing she would cry or scream at him or hit him. But she never did. She accepted it all without complaint.

"Are you mad at me, Jilly?"

She looked directly at him with clear blue eyes. "No, Daddy."

"Do you think I could have done something to save your mommy?"

"No."

"Or to keep you from getting hurt?"

She shook her head.

He turned his head as the waitress set down their plates, so she wouldn't see the tears in his eyes. When she left, he turned back to Jilly. She was sitting with her hands in her lap, looking solemnly down at her plate.

"Are you mad about the doll?" he whispered.

She looked up at him.

"The one I took away from you in Galveston?"

"It was a nice man that gave her to me. She was like me, Daddy, and I was going to take care of her."

Adam swallowed hard. "I—I was wrong to do that, Jilly. I should have let you keep it. I make lots of mistakes, honey. And that was one. I'm not asking you to forgive me for it. I just want you to know that I know I was wrong."

She leaned over and sucked loudly on the straw. She swallowed and said, "It's okay."

He leaned back, exhausted, and looked out the window. Jilly was calmly eating her grilled cheese sandwich, whereas he hadn't even touched his. He had no interest in food right now. And it bothered him that she did. Why didn't she yell at him for taking the doll away? Any other kid would have. But that was it, wasn't it? She wasn't any other kid. That was the thing that bothered him the most. He had been given a child who was not like all the rest. She accepted things that even an adult could not. She let life make its own reality. She didn't rant and rave and try to change it. At seven years old, she knew exactly who she was. Looking at her now, and loving her with all his heart, he wished almost desperately that he could be more like her.

"Is Erica going to come live with us?"

He took a drink of tea. "I—I don't know, honey."

"Do you want her to?"

"Do you?"

She set her sandwich down. "I asked you first, Daddy."

He smiled. "Yeah, you did, didn't you? Well, the truth is—I just don't know. I mean I do, but I'm just not sure." The way she was watching him made him feel like a babbling fool. "I really like to be with her."

"She's awful pretty, isn't she?"

"Yes, honey, she is. And sweet, too."

"You like to kiss her. I can tell."

He cleared his throat. "Yeah, you're right. I do."

Jilly sucked loudly on her shake. "Well, I hope she comes to live with us."

Adam sat back in his chair and smiled. That, he realized was what he had been waiting breathlessly to hear.

"Tomorrow is Christmas Eve, Daddy."

Christmas Eve. A day he had hoped would just slide right past him without making any impression was here. And he felt its glow all the way through his body. "Yes, honey, it is."

"Do you think Santa will remember me?"

He reached over and clasped her wrist, desperate to give her what she needed, desperate to have her forgive him and love him once again, desperate to let this season of giving return a tiny portion of their happiness. "I'm sure he will, honey."

"WELL, EVERYBODY," Larry was saying to the crew, "have a great holiday—that is, those of you who get the time off." There was a mixture of groans and applause from the mixed group. Some would get Christmas vacation and others would take New Year's.

The producer said a few words, offering his holiday blessings and his hopes for better ratings in the coming year.

When the group dispersed, Erica went back to her office to organize the files she wanted to work on over the holidays. She was only taking Christmas Eve and Christmas Day off, and she really didn't want to spend the time working, but she thought she'd better make some plans for next month's *Focal Point* programs.

Ever since that lunch the other day with her father, she had felt different, renewed. She felt as if she had just arrived from a very long, tedious journey. She had finally reached a place in her life that she could call her own. From here on out, she would make her own decisions and, if they were wrong ones, she would learn to live with them. And maybe—maybe someday her father would be able to see Adam and Jilly the way she did. There was always hope.

She closed her file drawer and turned around. Larry had folded out a chair on the opposite side of her desk and was sitting on it.

She jumped. "My gosh, Larry, you startled me!"

He folded his hands behind his neck and stretched back. "Sorry."

She set the files on her desk. "Well?"

"Well, what?"

She pursed her lips. "What do you want?"

"Can't I come in and wish my favorite lady in the whole world a merry Christmas?"

She glanced around the tiny office. "Where is my shovel?"

Larry chuckled and said, "Okay, sit down, kiddo."

Erica took a deep breath and sat down. She kept her hands in her lap, relaxed. For the first time since she came to work for the station, she wasn't clenching her fingers in anticipation of bad news.

"It's about the show."

Her voice was surprisingly calm, even to her. "*Focal Point*?"

"Yes."

"Okay, what?"

"They've decided to go with Manda."

"I see." A vague sort of numbness slid over her. She felt . . . nothing. It was a curious feeling, in a way. She didn't feel any sense of loss, any lack of self-esteem. Nothing.

"I don't want you to be upset now, babe."

"I'm not."

"Because that show the other day—the one at the hospital—was terrific. Miles and Bracken both said it was the best one the station has done."

"I think Jilly had a lot to do with that."

"Yeah, that kid was terrific. But it wasn't just her. No, Miles commented on how well you did. They want you to do more of that kind of thing. You know, the human interest gigs."

"No hard news, in other words."

He shook his head and looked sheepish. "No. They feel that—well, look we all know how gorgeous you are and—well, it's just that people see that face and think that you don't—"

Erica held up her hand. "Please, Larry. You don't have to tell me. I've lived with this face all my life."

"You look terrific on film."

"Yes."

"And you've got a great voice."

"Yes."

He shrugged. "But just not for the news. Not for the more hard-hitting interviews."

Erica glanced up at the fluorescent tube lighting above her and wondered what it was doing outside. Was it still warm and dry? Maybe she'd go for a walk. Maybe she'd go by and get Jilly and take her Christmas shopping.

"You're not quitting, are you?"

She lowered her gaze to Larry. "I'm not fired, is that right?"

"Are you kidding! Miles knows a commodity when he's got one, babe. And you are one helluva commodity. Tell me you're not quitting, 'cause I'll have a rotten holiday if I've got to hunt around for a replacement for you."

Her smile was a tired one. "You can relax, Larry. I'm not quitting. Not right now, anyway."

He let his breath out slowly. "So, you're not upset about the decision? I mean, they stuck me with this odious task and I've got to go back and tell them what you said."

"Tell them I think they're right, Larry. Tell them they made a wise decision."

"You don't want me to tell them that, babe."

"But it *was* a wise decision. I would be better at human interest pieces. I'm tired of the battles, Larry. I need a change."

Vastly relieved but confused by Erica's lack of fire, Larry stood up. He folded the chair and put it back into the corner. Before leaving, he gave her one last puzzled look. "There's more to you than I thought.

I—I thought I knew exactly who and what you were."
He smiled. "I guess I was wrong."

When he was gone, Erica locked her hands beneath
her chin and smiled. *I guess you were, Larry.*

## Chapter Fourteen

Erica juggled the packages in her arms and struggled to reach out and ring the doorbell. The door opened, and over the mound in her arms, she saw Adam's housekeeper.

"Hi, Etta."

"Oh, hello, miss. My, but you have a load. Let me help you there."

Erica let her take some of the packages and sighed in relief. "Thank you. I really shouldn't have tried to carry them all at once. These lazy man's loads are a bad habit of mine."

"Come in, come in," said Etta. "Can I make you a spot of tea?"

"That would be wonderful." She followed Etta into the kitchen. "Is Adam home?"

"No, he and the wee one went shopping." They set the packages down on the counter. Etta filled the kettle and put it on the burner. "Jilly was nearly beside herself. She had made a whole list of things she wanted to buy for people."

As disappointed as Erica was that Adam wasn't there, she was glad he was out doing something fun with Jilly. "Well, that's good."

Etta peered over at her knowingly. "They should be home before long. You and I can have a nice chat and then they should be here."

Erica smiled nervously. She liked Etta very much, but the woman scared her to death. After all, she had worked for years for Adam's wife. She had practically raised Jilly. Now here Erica was, an interloper into the family. Etta probably saw her as someone trying to wheedle her way into Adam's affections, displacing the former wife from her rightful place.

While Etta worked on the tea, Erica looked around. The kitchen was once again spotless. A few herbs sat in pots on the windowsill, but the garden beyond the window lay fallow.

"Mrs. Bech must have been an avid gardener."

Etta's gaze followed Erica's out the window. "Oh, she loved the garden, she did. Loved havin' all those jars of fresh vegetables in the pantry. We have so much left on the shelves and Mr. B. didn't seem to show any interest in the garden, so we've just let it go." Her voice grew sad. "But I do so like to see green things agrowin'. The yard used to be just bursting with color."

Erica's nerves stretched tighter. She watched Etta pour the tea into two cups and she brought them to the table.

"I can use a spot myself," she said, sitting down. "I'm all finished for the day anyway. I have a chicken soup on the stove for them, but Mrs. Grobinski called a bit ago and invited them to dinner tonight. So I may just pop the soup into the fridge."

"Oh, they're going to his partner's house? Tonight?"

"I imagine they will. Jilly loves to go there."

The disappointment grew more acute. She was so hoping to do something with Adam and Jilly again. Maybe order another pizza. Just be a family, even if it was only pretend. She longed for their kind of life, for a normal family existence. But maybe she was expecting too much too soon. Adam and Jilly had each other. They had set up the structure in which they lived a long time ago. When Jilly's mother was still alive. Adam's wife.

Erica took a sip of the hot tea. "This is delicious. I won't stay long. I only wanted to drop off these packages and—"

"Mr. B. would be mighty disappointed if you were gone when he comes back."

Erica stared at the housekeeper. "Oh, I don't think he—"

"It may not be any of my say-so, but I can see a change in the man. I think you've had something to do with it."

Erica smiled thinly. "I'm not trying to change him. I just—"

"It's for the better. He's been a sad creature, miss. He's been swimming around in his grief too long. He needs somebody to give 'im a good shake. I've tried a time or two, but—he needs a woman like yourself. And my little Jilly needs someone, too." Her penetrating gaze narrowed on Erica's face. "You feel somethin' for the little one?"

"Oh, I do. I—I don't know exactly how it happened, but she has just—just wormed her way into my heart."

Etta smiled. "She has a way of doing that, she does. She's a special one."

"It would be hard not to love Jilly."

Etta wrapped her fingers around the warm cup and nodded slowly. "She's got some hard times ahead of her, though."

"Is she—well, Adam has never talked about it much, but is she going to have to have more surgery?"

"That, she is. She goes to doctors all the time for this and that. It's a long road back from the place she's been. And for Mr. B., too." She looked at Erica. "It'll take a strong woman to handle all that…if one should choose to do so."

Erica took a deep breath. "Etta, I—I don't want you to think that I'm trying to take Mrs. Bech's place or anything. But—well, I really care about Adam and Jilly. And I think they care about me, too." She looked down at the cup in front of her. "I'm just not sure I'm strong enough to be what they need."

"That Mr. Bech, he's a good judge of people. He lost his way there for a while, but he knows what he's doin'. If he thinks good things about you, then there are good things there for the rest of us to see, too."

Erica's smile relaxed for the first time. "Thank you, Etta. I hope, if nothing else, that you and I will become friends."

"Well," said Etta. "I believe we already are."

WHEN ADAM AND JILLY came home, Etta and Erica were in the living room, putting the packages Erica had brought around the base of the tree.

Jilly came running into the living room from the kitchen. "Hi, Erica! We went shopping. Oh, who are those for?"

Etta patted her on the bottom. "Never you mind, now. Y'know what curiosity did to the cat."

"No, what?"

"Killed it."

Jilly's eyes widened. "Really?" She turned to her dad. "Really?"

Adam smiled and shook his head, but his attention was focused solely on Erica. She was on her knees in front of the tree, her hair pulled back in clips, and wearing a green knit jumpsuit that made her blue eyes sparkle. All he did was think about her, want her, wish she was here. And now here she was. In his house, next to his Christmas tree, giving his daughter an affectionate hug, then gazing up at him with a look that was filled with—did he dare ask for that much? It was wishful thinking, that was all. A last-minute Christmas wish. He should be happy with what he had. She had already given Jilly and him so much.

"Hi, Adam. I—I had a few things I wanted to drop off."

He knelt down beside her. His hand looped around the back of her neck. "I'm glad you did." Realizing there were two other people in the room watching him devour Erica with his eyes, he cleared his throat and stood up. "We've been out shopping."

She grinned at the load he had set down. "I see that."

He stacked the packages under the tree. Some he set aside. "I've got to get these over to Dub's."

"They've invited you to dinner, sir," said Etta.

"Who has?"

"Mr. and Mrs. Grobinski."

"For tonight?"

"Yes, sir. At seven, the missus said." Etta leaned down to Jilly. "And they said they had a special little somethin' for you."

"They do! What?"

Etta backed up and raised her arms. "I don't know. I just mind my own business around here." She grinned at Erica. "And now I must be on my way."

Jilly threw her arms around Etta. "Do you have to go? Can't you stay here for Christmas?"

Etta patted her back, then set her aside. "And what would my own family think of that? They'd starve to death." She turned to Adam. "I'm going to put some soup in the fridge for you to have this week and then I'll be on my way."

Adam pulled an envelope from his pocket and handed it over to her. "Thank you, Etta. And have a very merry Christmas."

"I will do that, sir. And to you."

"Wait, Etta!" Jilly cried. She bent over and picked up a small package, carrying it over to the house-keeper. "This is from me."

Etta took the gift and held it next to her heart. "It will be the first one I open on Christmas morning." She bent down and kissed Jilly's cheek. "Merry Christmas, little one."

"Merry Christmas, Etta."

"And to you, miss."

Erica smiled at her, glad that she had found another good friend in this house. "Thank you, Etta. For everything."

"Not to mention it." She walked past a puzzled Adam and into the kitchen. Jilly trailed behind her, trying to get her to guess what was in the package.

Adam grabbed Erica's hand and pulled her to her feet and then up against him. His arms looped around her back. She fit perfectly against his body, softly conforming and oh, so warm. "What was that all about?'' he whispered against her temple, then let his mouth slide down to her neck.

Her eyes closed and she smiled to herself. "Just girl talk.''

"That's what you and Jilly said yesterday."

"Well, there's a lot of that going on around here these days.''

His mouth trailed over her cheek and toward her lips. "Well," he breathed against her, "this is man-woman talk." He touched her lips with his, piercingly gentle, his hand trailing down over her hips and hauling her into the wedge of his body. He had to force himself to restrain from pulling her down to the floor and doing what his body ached to do, what it had ached to do since the last time he made love to her.

She nibbled the lobe of his ear, and he felt as if he would melt into one big puddle on the floor. "God, I've missed you!"

"You just saw me this afternoon."

He let his fingers sift through the gold strands of her hair. "No, I mean I've missed you." His hand slid down her neck and throat and onto the front of her sweater. "I wish we didn't have to go anywhere for dinner. I wish we could just stay here together, all night long.''

"But you can't. You have to go to dinner."

He pulled back and wrapped his hand around her arm and slid it up and down. "I want you to go with us.''

"I wasn't invited, Adam."

"I'm inviting you."

She smiled. "You're not having the dinner party."

"They told me—Dub told me if I wanted to bring you to dinner sometime, I could. Well, I do."

"You told him about me?"

He ran his hand through her hair, studying each strand that sifted through his fingers. "Dub and I have been friends for a long time. I can't hide much from him."

Her hands rested on his chest. "What did you tell him?"

He twisted a gold strand of hair around his finger and smiled. "Oh, I didn't have to say much. He could just tell. That glint in my eye, I guess."

She slapped his chest playfully. "Can't you control yourself in public better than that?"

"Not when I'm thinking of you."

She sighed. "What on earth am I going to do with you, Adam?"

"Well," he said, trailing a finger down the center of her sweater and following the journey with his eyes. "How about falling in love with me?"

Her breath collapsed in her throat. "I—I think I've already done that," she managed in a whisper. "What comes next?"

His lips parted to say something, but Jilly burst into the room. "Can we go to Dub's now, Daddy?"

He reluctantly loosened his hold on Erica. "We'll go in a little while. Why don't you decide what you want to wear."

"I want Erica to help me."

"Okay," she said. "I tell you what. You get started and I'll be right there."

Jilly left to pick out an outfit and Adam turned to Erica. "You will go with us, won't you?"

She hedged. "I don't know, Adam."

"I want them to get to know you."

"You said Dub told you to bring me, but what about his wife?"

Adam sighed and pushed his hands into the pockets of his slacks. "I want Mo to get to know you, too."

"Was she good friends with your wife?"

Adam looked at her and nodded. "They were best friends."

Erica felt like a balloon that had just been punctured. "Oh, Adam, then I can't go to their house for dinner. And especially not at Christmas."

He reached for her. "You can, Erica. You'll be with me. Mo is a good woman. She'll accept that."

Erica still hesitated, not sure she was ready to face yet another emotional battle.

But Adam reached for her and said, "I want you with me, Erica." He grinned. "You want me to be able to behave in public, don't you?"

"You need me along that badly, huh?"

He touched her ear with his lips. "In the worst way."

THE IMPOSING HOUSE sat on a quiet cul-de-sac that sloped down to the bayou below. They stepped out of the car, but Erica hung back. Adam paused and smiled encouragingly at her. "Come on, Erica. Don't chicken out on me now. Goodness, I would have thought there was never a place where you didn't belong."

She sighed heavily. "I'm not so sure I belong here." She looked at him. "Or in your wife's house."

Jilly was hurrying up the sidewalk and around to the back door. Adam's eyes darkened. "That was a cheap shot, Erica."

"It's meant to be the truth."

He leaned forward and whispered angrily, "You don't know anything about my marriage."

Erica glanced up at the starlit sky. She looked back at Adam and said quietly, "That's because you haven't chosen to tell me anything."

He rested his hand on the top of the car and sighed. "What do you want to know, Erica? I was married for ten years. Her name was Marilyn. She died."

She glared at him. "Why are you being flip with me?"

He grabbed her and, enveloping her in his arms, held her close, his face against her hair. "I'm sorry, Erica. I'm really—sorry. This has got me a little uptight, too. It's not an easy night for me, either."

Erica pulled back and looked into his face. "You're afraid?"

He shrugged. "Yeah, I am."

"Is it that you're worried what their reaction will be? To me? To us?"

He nodded and ran his hands up and down her sides. "For ten years, people have seen me a certain way. As part of a couple. Marilyn and Adam. Adam and Marilyn." He leaned back against the car, one arm still looped around her waist. "And then one of us died. One of us is left. And . . . and I was the driver of the boat."

"Oh, Adam, you don't think—" She laid her hands on each side of his face. "You don't think they blame you, do you?"

"Sometimes, my friends look at me with this—this look. It's sort of like pity and it's sort of like . . . like why her and not you?"

"I don't believe that. I don't believe that anyone would think that."

"Yeah? Well, now you sound like the therapist we go to. Oh, I'm an interesting specimen, all right. Here I am in one chair, the guilt-ridden husband and father, and there's Jilly, the one they can't crack, the one who accepts it all with grace and dignity." He tried to smile at her. "I'm a real pain in the neck, Erica. I hope you realize that."

She smiled back. "Oh, I realize it all right." She stood on tiptoe and kissed his nose. "I also know, Adam, how well you take away all those pains."

He kissed her hard then, parting her lips with his tongue, one arm looped around her, the other hand moving up to cover her breast. The front porch light came on and the door opened.

They pulled apart and looked guiltily at the rectangle of light. Dub and Mo stood side by side in the center of it. On Dub's face was a crooked smile. Mo stood more stiffly, her expression blank. Erica felt like a complete fool. Adam, she knew, had to feel the same.

Jilly wedged between the Grobinskis. "Come on, Daddy. I've been in here for a long time."

Adam kept his arm wrapped around Erica's back and waist and smiled down at her. "Well," he said, breathing deeply, "here we go."

As nervous as she was, Erica knew that they were in this together. For the first time in her life, she knew she was not alone anymore.

AFTER FIVE MINUTES in their home, Erica felt that Dub Grobinski was an old friend. As soon as she walked in the door with Adam, Dub pulled her to him and wrapped his big, strong arm around her. He was not a particularly attractive man, but there was something about him, an aura of sorts, that was captivating.

"I'm just tickled that Adam brought you with him tonight," said Dub. "I get so tired of always looking at his ugly mug. Now I get to have two gorgeous women across the table from me tonight."

Erica laughed and turned to Mo. Adam introduced them. "Erica, this is my good friend, big sister, and all-around worrywart, Mo. Mo, this is Erica Manning."

Erica's dazzling smile was often threatening to women. It had served her well in the past, but tonight she tried to temper it. "I appreciate your letting me come. I know it was short notice."

"Not at all," said Mo, stretching her hand out. "Any friend of Adam's is welcome here." Her smile was wide, her voice polite, but Erica could feel a certain insecurity wavering in the words.

"Come on in," said Dub. "Let's have a drink." He scooped Jilly up in his arms and carried her into the living room, setting her down by the tree. He grinned at the girl. "Now, I do believe that somewhere here— Where did we put that lump of coal, Mo?"

Jilly sat waiting excitedly but patiently until Dub located a tiny package under the tree.

"Well, here it is." He handed it over to her.

She looked up at him, her eyes wide. "Is it really a lump of coal?"

He blustered. "Well now, I can't tell you what's inside there. That would ruin the surprise, wouldn't it?"

She carried the box over to Adam. "Will you help me, Daddy?"

Adam took it in his hands, and they all watched as Jilly worked the bow and paper loose. Erica held her breath as the child struggled, wanting to rush over and help her but realizing, as they all did, that she needed to do this herself.

Erica glanced at Adam's face. He was gazing at Jilly, his eyes liquid and bright, a soft smile on his face. He was a man who had so much love inside of him for his child. Looking at the sweet little girl in front of him, it was easy to understand why.

Jilly pried open the box and squealed in delight. She pulled out a small glass angel that hung from a piece of gold thread.

"It's like yours!" she exclaimed, running over to the tree to compare it with the one she had admired a few weeks ago.

"Just like it." Mo smiled.

Jilly ran back over and showed it to her dad.

"It's beautiful, honey," he said, hugging her tightly to his chest. "Just like my own little angel."

"Look, Erica. Isn't it pretty?"

"It's beautiful."

"Will you help me hang it on our tree later?"

"We'll put it right in the front where everybody can see it."

Erica gave Jilly a big hug, aware that everyone in the room was watching her. It was another test, she knew. She glanced over at Adam and he smiled tenderly at her.

Jilly showed her angel to everyone in the room so they could all admire it, and then the gift exchange began. Mo found a scarf from Adam and Jilly. And Adam opened a bottle of 1960 Château Lafite-Rothschild.

When he insisted that the gift was too much, Dub waved his hand and said, "Oh, that old thing's just been gathering dust in my cellar."

Adam laughed. "That's what it's supposed to do, Dub."

"Well, you just save that for a special occasion and then enjoy it."

Dub opened his cigars that Adam had found in Galveston and grinned sheepishly at Mo.

"Now why on earth would you buy these for me?" asked Dub, feigning total innocence.

Mo gave him a playful slap on the arm. "Just don't you light one of those in this house."

Dub leaned over and kissed her on the cheek, smiling. "Whatever you say, dear."

Erica and Adam exchanged a smile. It was easy to see that Dub and Mo had a very special relationship. Erica only hoped that someday she too could share that kind of love with someone. She wondered what it would be like to grow old with Adam, to share the little moments of life together. She thought there was nothing in the world she would want as much as that.

Adam reached for her hand and pulled her over closer to him on the couch. He wrapped his arm around her.

Mo stood up and stretched. "I'll go see how dinner is doing."

Erica jumped up. "Let me help you."

Mo's smile was hesitant and a little shy, but she nodded and said, "All right."

Erica followed her into a bright, spacious kitchen. "What can I do to help?"

"Well, I guess you can help with the salad." She got the things out of the refrigerator and set them on the counter for Erica. They began working together, quietly, each unsure yet of where the other stood.

Mo glanced over at her. "I can see why Adam has fallen for you. You've very beautiful."

Erica smiled thinly, nervously. "What makes you think Adam has fallen for me?"

She smiled knowingly. "Believe me, I've known Adam for a long, long time. I saw the way he was looking at you." She shrugged. "Besides, Dub told me." She looked sideways at Erica. "Is it serious?"

Erica unscrewed the lid to the jar of olives and stared down at the counter. "For me, it is." She glanced at Mo. "I hope you don't think I'm some sort of intruder. I understand you and Adam's wife were very close."

Mo's hands flattened on the counter and she leaned her weight into them. "We were," she said quietly. "I still have trouble believing that she's gone."

"It must be so hard for Jilly and Adam," said Erica. She wasn't really sure she wanted Mo to agree with her. She didn't want to hear how miserable Adam was without his wife.

"Jilly especially. You know," said Mo, "I probably shouldn't say this, but—well, she's like a granddaughter to me and I feel that I have to stand up for her."

Erica smiled. "I don't mind. I'm glad someone wants to stand up for her."

Mo gave Erica a long, appraising look. "You know, when I first saw you, I wondered if this was one of those fly-by-night things. But when I saw you out there with Jilly tonight, I knew there was something special and—and permanent there."

"Jilly brings the best out in people."

"Yes," said Mo. "But only if there is the best to bring out."

Erica smiled, grateful for the compliment.

"But what I was going to say," Mo continued, "is that Jilly has special needs, which could be trying at times. I want you to know that I'm always here to help. And Dub, too. I hope Adam realizes that."

"I'll tell him that. Should I set this on the table?"

"Yes, please do."

Erica pushed through the door into the dining room and set the salad on the table. She had been so afraid to come here tonight to meet the Grobinskis. And, she had to admit, she still wasn't sure she had aced the test. But she really liked Mo. There was something very honest and good-hearted about her. Even if she had been Marilyn's best friend, Erica still felt that there was a tiny bit of room left in Mo's heart for her.

She went back into the kitchen. "What now?"

"Stick that French bread in the oven, will you, please?"

"Sure."

"Anyway," said Mo, as if the conversation had never been interrupted, "I'm glad Adam has found someone. I've been awfully worried about him, you know. This whole thing has been so hard on him."

Erica stuck the bread in the oven. "He tries to hide his pain."

Mo took a deep breath and shook her head, thinking of the past. "Adam used to be the most likable man I've ever known," she said, looking directly at Erica. "Everyone thought so. He was funny and kind and—well, you know how handsome he is."

"He is that."

The two women grinned.

"Things were not perfect between Marilyn and him." She shrugged. "But I'm sure he's told you that."

Erica tried to keep her mouth from falling open.

"Of course, Adam was the type of man who would never let it show. He was always kind to her, always loving, always a gentleman. I don't think Marilyn ever regretted marrying him. Not for a minute."

Erica thought of Adam, sitting out in the living room with Dub. She understood completely what Mo was saying. And she knew, for a fact, that she would never, ever regret the time they'd had together—the loving times, the debating times, the times with Jilly when Erica felt as if she had a family of her own.

"Thank you for letting Adam bring me tonight, Mo."

Mo lifted the platter of meat to carry to the table. She turned and smiled at Erica. "Anytime, Erica. I have a feeling we're going to be seeing quite a bit of each other."

"WHAT A NIGHT," Erica said, sighing and smiling as she rested her head against Adam's couch.

Adam sat beside her, his arm resting on the back of the couch, a tired smile on his face. "That bad?" he said, running his hand through her hair.

With her head still down, she turned toward him. "No, it was wonderful. I mean that. They are really fine people."

"They are, aren't they?" He leaned over and moved his mouth lightly over hers. "They were taken with you, too." His mouth moved to the side of her ear. "Can't say that I blame them."

Erica rested her hand against his chest. "We have to talk, Adam."

He tried to move his mouth against her ear again. "I thought that's what we were doing. Jilly's in bed and—"

"I'm serious."

His hand fell to the back of the couch. "I know. That's what scares me."

"I want you to tell me about your wife, Adam."

"She's dead."

"Please. Please, Adam," she said, moving her fingers along the side of his throat. "I have to know where I stand."

He had trouble concentrating when she touched him, but he didn't have the will to move her hand away. "You're not competing with a ghost, if that's what you're wondering."

"I'm wondering what you felt, Adam. I want to know you. Your marriage was a big part of you. Can't you understand that?"

His eyes closed, and his focus was centered on that spot on his throat where her hand rested. His hand came up and grasped her fingers, pulling them up to his lips. "I think I love you, Erica." His words were breathed into her palm. "I haven't felt this kind of love for a long time. Many years."

He opened his eyes and brought her hand to his chest, still gripping it tightly between his fingers. "Please try to understand. Marilyn was the mother of my child. She was my wife for ten years. Those things will never be forgotten." He sighed again. "But, if we're talking about love, the kind you read about and daydream about . . . it wasn't that kind."

She looped her free hand around the back of his neck. "I'm not trying to pry into your life, Adam. I just want to know you. I want to know everything about you."

He pulled her against him. "I feel the same way about you, Erica, but...I don't know, I feel this urgency—as if time is running out for me. Why do I feel that way? It's so scary."

Her fingers threaded through his hair, and she kissed the side of his neck. "I think it's probably natural to feel that way when you've been through something like you have."

He pulled back and looked down at her earnestly, almost feverishly. "But I don't know what to do about it. I want so much with you. I want it now. I want to ask you to marry me, but—"

"Is that what you feel you *should* do?"

His hands grasped the side of her face, and his thumb stroked the rim of her lips. "I want you with me. I want that so badly."

"I'm here, Adam."

"But you might go away."

"And you think by asking me to marry you, it's going to keep me here?"

His thumb followed the line of her chin, mapping out a course along her skin. "Maybe. I don't know. I want to do the right thing. For you. For Jilly....for me."

"Maybe neither one of us is ready—emotionally— for marriage."

"You make me feel so good, Erica. So whole again. I didn't think I'd ever feel this way. You're so special."

"You're the one who's made me that way," she said with a soft smile. "All my life I've been nothing but a pretty shell, perfect on the outside, empty on the inside."

He shook his head. "No, you were just hiding way back in there, like a snail that was afraid to come out."

"Way, way back," she said, then sighed, her eyes trailing down the planes of his handsome face, landing at his mouth. "I love you, Adam. I've never known love like this before."

He leaned forward and his tongue slowly circled the line of her lips. "Then, let's get married," he whispered against her mouth.

Her eyes closed and she felt herself drifting down into the solid basin of his arms. His hand slid up the front of her jumpsuit slowly, gliding from the top of her thigh to her breast. She tried to find her breath. "It would be so easy to say yes."

"Then do."

"I think we have a way to go, Adam. I think Jilly has a way to go before she's ready for a new mother."

His kiss became more urgent, and his fingers fumbled with her buttons, pushing aside the material. "What if I can't wait? Would you turn me down if I asked you?"

She let him lower her to the couch, and his mouth slid down over her chin, down her throat and onto her breast.

"No," she moaned. "I wouldn't turn you down."

His voice was hoarse and dry with aching need. "Will you come to my bed?"

She tried to find her breath. "Yes."

He stood up and lifted her from the couch. His hands moved insistently over her and her mouth remained fastened to his.

"I don't think I can make it to the bed," he whispered, his hand holding her hips tightly against him. He lowered her slowly to the floor, dancing lights from the Christmas tree playing over their clothes. He moved against her as they fumbled with each other's clothes, yanking them off as quickly as they could. When they lay in a heap nearby, he lay over her, his fingers moving into her, his heated gaze filling her with desire as he looked down at her. "Did I tell you I love you?" he whispered, lowering himself into her.

"Yes," she moaned breathlessly, pulling his mouth down to hers. "But tell me again."

## Chapter Fifteen

On Christmas morning, when Erica opened her eyes, she was aware of a rustle of movement beside her bed in the guest room. The figure was small and blond and wearing a blue cotton nightgown. Erica sat up and her eyes slowly began to focus.

"Hi, Erica."

She smiled sleepily. "Good morning, Jilly."

"I'm glad you slept over."

Erica's body still sizzled from the memories of the past two nights with Adam. His hands, the heat from his body, the way he felt inside her. She stretched languorously. "Yes, so am I." She glanced out the window. The sun was just peeking over the horizon, promising another beautiful day. She knew, without opening the window, that it would be warm outside, that there would be no snow, no Currier and Ives.

She smiled to herself. But that no longer mattered. This was a day like no other. Perfect and pristine.

She reached out and pulled Jilly onto the bed with her. "Merry Christmas, honey."

Jilly sat Indian-style on the bed and pulled the blanket up over her, smiling. "Merry Christmas. Let's go see if Santa came."

"Don't you think we should wait for your father?"

"I'm up. I'm up." Leaning against the doorjamb was Adam, wearing a faded gray sweat suit. He rubbed his head sleepily.

Jilly twirled around on the bed, a hopeful expression on her face. "Merry Christmas, Daddy."

He came into the room, his gaze shifting lovingly from Erica to the little girl on her bed. He sat down, one hand resting on Erica's ankle, covered by the bedspread, and the other reaching out to take Jilly's hand.

"Merry Christmas, honey bunch." He pulled her into his lap, then focused all of his attention on Erica. Her hair was tousled about her face and she wore no makeup. He thought he had never seen anyone look so beautiful in the morning in his life.

He smiled at her. "Am I going to get to wake up to this vision of loveliness every morning?" He leaned over and, with Jilly still in his lap, kissed Erica soundly on the mouth.

"Are you gonna be sleeping over every night, Erica?"

Adam set her on the floor and patted her bottom. "We've got lots of time to discuss all that. What I want to do is go see if Santa brought me anything."

"Oh, Daddy, you're too old for Santa Claus."

He laid one hand on Erica's leg and the other against Jilly's face, and shook his head. "I don't think so. I've been given the best gift in the world."

"What's that?" Jilly wanted to know.

"The love of two very special ladies, that's what."

"Oh," said Jilly, wiggling out of his arms.

"Oh," whispered Erica, smiling at him.

"Hurry and get dressed, you lazybones," teased Adam. "It's Santy Claus time."

Erica threw back the covers and laughed. "Then get out of my way."

Adam scooped up Jilly and took her out of the guest bedroom. "Let's go get your robe, sweetie. Maybe old slowpoke will be ready by then."

Erica stood up and stretched, feeling happier than she had ever felt in her life. Was this the way it was always going to be with these two people? Would every day bring such hope and joy?

She was realistic enough to know that there would be some rough seas ahead, that life was not all smooth sailing. But today was Christmas Day, and at least for now, her world was filled with hope and love and an almost achingly sweet sense of contentment.

When she had washed her face and dressed once again in her green jumpsuit, she ran a brush quickly through her hair. "I'm ready," she called, coming out into the hall. Adam held Jilly in his arms, and they were both leaning against the wall, snoring loudly and pretending to be asleep.

"All right, you wise guys. Let's go tear up that wrapping paper."

Adam and Jilly glanced at each other and laughed. Together, the three of them hurried down the long hall and on down the stairs, eager to rip into the packages.

Erica knew that back at her apartment there would be a present from her father. And she knew that it would be an exquisite piece of jewelry or a lovely art object. There would be nothing personal in the gift, no trace of her father's love. But that was okay. She had faith that he would learn, just as she had learned, to find the beauty in Adam and Jilly. Someday she hoped he too would find beauty beneath the facade.

"Do I dare suggest that we make some coffee first?" Adam asked.

"No!" cried Erica and Jilly at the same time.

He shrugged. "I didn't think so."

They rounded the corner into the den. The room was definitely Erica's favorite. It was warm and cozy and so very much like Adam.

Jilly ran to the fireplace. "Santa's been here!"

"He has?" marveled Adam. "Well, he sure has. And he ate those cookies you left for him, too."

"And he drank the milk!"

"No wonder he's so fat," said Adam.

Jilly stared at the dollhouse that sat on the hearth. "Is this for me!"

"Well, gosh," said Adam. "I don't know. Maybe it's for me."

"Oh, Daddy. You don't play with dollhouses."

"Oh, yeah, I forgot."

She ran over and hugged Adam. "I'm so glad Santa didn't forget me." She hurried back over to her stocking. "And look at all this candy!"

She poured it out onto the hearth and stuck something into her mouth.

"Bubble gum for breakfast?" Erica cried, grimacing.

"Don't knock it," said Adam. "If I forgot to go to the store, we may be having leftover pizza."

Jilly ran to the tree. "Can I pass out the gifts?"

"Of course you can, honey." He clapped his hands. "Come on, let's get the show on the road."

Jilly sat beneath the tree, reaching for one package after another.

"Hey," complained Adam good-naturedly, "How come they're all for you?"

"'Cause I'm more pop'lar than you."

"Well, I guess so."

Erica curled up on the couch, while Adam sat in his favorite chair.

"Get that one over there, Jilly-girl, the one in red."

Jilly crawled beneath the tree and dragged out a huge package wrapped in shiny red paper. "It says 'To Erica, from Adam.' It's from you, Daddy!"

"How about that. Hand it over to the lady, will you?"

"How come it's so big and flat?" asked Jilly.

"Somebody must have sat on it." Adam laughed.

Jilly scrambled over to Erica, dragging the package behind her.

Erica looked long and hard at the present before curiosity got the best of her and she pulled it into her lap and tore at the package.

She stared down at the painting in her lap. "Currier and Ives?" she marveled. "Where did you get this? How did you know?"

He grinned. "Oh, I have my sources."

"Dad?" she asked in disbelief.

"Well—" Adam shrugged "—he's trying. I appreciated the hint."

She shook her head, amazed at the way life worked. Who would have thought even a month ago that she would be sitting here with Adam Bech and his daughter, sharing the most meaningful experience of her life. And that her father, who was so against this relationship and what it meant for his daughter's future, could contribute to it in such a subtle way.

Erica climbed off the couch and leaned over Adam's chair. Her mouth met his in a warm embrace. "This is wonderful, Adam. Thank you so much."

"Just wanted you to feel like it was Christmas."

She glanced at Jilly, rummaging for packages under the tree. She smiled softly at Adam. "How could I not feel that it is Christmas? To be here with you—every day would be Christmas."

He breathed deeply, pulling her down into the chair, next to him. She snuggled against his body, secure and warm in his arms.

Erica called to Jilly. "Honey, get that box—that gold one there."

Jilly pulled it out from under the tree. "'To Adam from Erica,'" she read. She brought it to him.

"This must be for me." He grinned.

Erica shifted her weight so he could open the package.

He opened the lid on the box and pulled out a beautiful shell. He smiled softly at Erica.

She touched it. "I'm way down in there somewhere."

He lifted her hand and kissed it. "Good. I'll take it to work, then I'll always have you with me."

Sitting together in the chair, they watched Jilly opening her presents. Adam lavished the gifts on her, and she seemed delighted with each and every one.

"Is this from you, Erica?"

Erica grinned at her. "Well, what does the tag say?"

Jilly read. "It says 'To my best friend, Jilly. From Erica.'"

"Then I guess that one's from me."

Jilly tore into the box. Inside was a white chiffon dress.

Jilly pulled it out and stared reverently at it. "It's so beautiful!"

"I was seven when I wore that, Jilly. Just your size."

Jilly spun around with the dress held in front of her. "Did you wear it in one of your beauty contests?"

"Uh-huh."

"Wow!" breathed Jilly. She turned toward her father. "Isn't it pretty, Daddy?"

He smiled at her. "You are beautiful, Jilly. It's perfect for you."

Jilly came over to the big chair and threw her arms around Erica. Adam wrapped his arms around both of them, pulling Jilly into his lap beside Erica.

"My two girls," he said with a smile. "Merry Christmas, ladies."

"Merry Christmas!" They laughed, hugging each other.

"I think we should eat some breakfast," Adam suggested.

"Leftover pizza?" asked Erica.

"Well...maybe there's something else."

Jilly and Erica climbed off Adam's lap and pulled him to his feet.

"It's worked, hasn't it, Erica?" asked Jilly, a big smile on her face.

"What's that?"

"All the hugs and kisses."

Erica took an assessment of Adam's bemused expression. "Yes, Jilly, I believe it has."

Adam wrapped his arm around Erica, and they started for the kitchen.

At Jilly's gasp, Adam and Erica jerked and turned around. They stared toward the far corner of the room where Jilly was pointing.

Adam's gaze narrowed on the object in the corner. "What—what on earth!"

Erica stared, dumbfounded.

Jilly moved toward the corner slowly, tentatively, her eyes wide with amazement.

Adam turned to Erica with a look of wonder in his face. "How on earth—how did you do that!"

Erica's eyes were wide with shock. She turned to Adam in amazement. "You didn't throw it away after all?"

"The dolly!" whispered Jilly, her voice filled with wonderment and awe. She reached the corner, kneeling down to gingerly scoop it up in her arms. "Daddy...it's here!" she whispered tearfully. She turned around with the doll held tightly against her chest. "He brought it, Daddy. Santa brought it to me!"

Erica's surprised grin turned to a frown when she noticed the look on Adam's face. "Why are you looking at me like that?" she whispered. "I can't believe you did this! You are so sneaky!"

Now it was his turn to frown. His voice, too, was a low whisper. He shook his head. "No. You mean—

Erica, do you mean to tell me you didn't rescue the doll from the trash?"

She glanced over at Jilly, cradling the doll under her chin. "No," she whispered, stupefied. "Adam..."

She thought back to that day in Galveston. She remembered distinctly the way the old man had come over to Jilly, making faces at her, making her laugh. He had smiled down at her with that toothless grin, his eyes directed solely at her—as if Erica wasn't even there.

"Adam..."

He looked back over at the corner. Jilly was still hugging the doll, kissing its cheeks and rocking it against her chest.

Something filled Adam's mind and body—a new emotion—a sense of wonder and joy that had been absent forever, it seemed. He looked at Erica in amazement, filled with new light, new hope, and an indescribable joy.

Wrapping his arms around Erica, he held her tight against him, cradling all the love and happiness she had brought into his house. "Merry Christmas, my love," he breathed against her lips.

Erica savored the taste of his mouth over hers. She had given up so long ago believing in miracles. Christmas had become just another holiday, another day off from work. She knew she would never feel that way about it again. Miracles really did happen. And the greatest miracle of her life was having the tender love of a man like Adam and a very special, unconditional love from a child like Jilly.

"Merry Christmas, Adam."

His mouth moved to her ear. "Grow old with me, Erica."

"I will, Adam," she whispered lovingly, holding him close. "This is forever."

The last barrier fell away from his heart and he felt at peace, knowing that once again he had a future filled with love and happiness.

# *Epilogue*

Adam gently lay Jilly down on the bed, and Erica covered her with her favorite green blanket.

"It's March, honey," he said. "Don't you think it's getting a little warm for this?"

Jilly snuggled into the covers. "I don't care. I like to be cozy."

"It was a big day, wasn't it?" asked Erica, smiling down at the girl.

"You were the prettiest bride I've ever seen, Erica."

Erica brushed the hair back from the little girl's face. "And you were the prettiest flower girl I've ever known."

"I'm glad you live with us now," she said sleepily.

"So am I. Good night, Jilly."

"Good night, Erica."

Erica moved out of the room, pausing in the doorway for a brief moment to look back at the man and child she had chosen to join as a family. Her heart swelled with joy at the sight, and she said a silent prayer of thanks for the precious gift she had been given.

She went down the hallway to the bedroom she and Adam would now share. Boxes of her clothes were piled in one corner. There would be plenty of time to put them away. She wasn't going to rush anything. She and Adam both had the rest of their lives together. They had worked so hard to make it to this moment. Now she was going to savor and cherish each second slowly and purposefully. They had each other. Forever.

ADAM SAT DOWN on the edge of Jilly's bed and pulled the covers up under her chin. "Are you happy, honey?"

She sighed. "Oh, yes. Why did you and Erica take so long to get married?"

He smiled. "We just wanted to make sure it was right for all of us."

"I'm glad she's here with us."

"So am I, darlin'."

"It's kinda neat that my best friend is my mom, too."

"You're a really lucky kid."

She snuggled in deeper. "Yeah, I know."

"I love you, sweetheart."

Jilly's eyes were heavy and sleepy, but she was still able to pull up a smile for her daddy. "I love you, too."

He kissed her forehead and stood up, heading for the door. "I love you more."

"I love you ten times more."

"A million times more."

"Infinity times more."

She pulled the blanket up to her chin, her face softening in contentment. "Infinity plus one."

Adam smiled, peace and happiness drifting down over him like a down comforter. This was his life now. The old one was not forgotten, but it was behind him. He had a wonderful little girl and a wife whom he loved to distraction. Together they would all build a new family, a new life. He was no longer looking for perfection. Now he knew that having love was enough.

"Daddy?" she called sleepily.

Adam turned around in the doorway. "Yes, honey?"

"How come you don't leave the light on in the hall anymore?"

Adam felt the glow of warmth fill his mind and body. He smiled into the darkened room. "Well, Jilly-girl, I don't need the light anymore. You turned it back on inside of me. You gave me all the light I need. That's the one that will keep me safe. The only one I need."

"I did that?"

"Yes, Jilly, you did."

She smiled sleepily. "I'm glad, Daddy."

"So am I, honey. So am I."

# H A R L E Q U I N
## *American Romance*®

## COMING NEXT MONTH

### #373 HEARTS AT RISK by Libby Hall

Reporting for an underground newspaper, Jennifer Wright champions counterculture causes—and fears love's dangers. Test pilot Lij Brannigan explores the limits of speed and performance in experimental jets—and struggles with his own demons. And on the day man takes his first step on the moon, the antiestablishment journalist and the fearless top gun enter an unknown world— one that mingles age-old desire and space-age conflict. Don't miss the next A CENTURY OF AMERICAN ROMANCE book!

### #374 LAZARUS RISING by Anne Stuart

Though Katharine Lafferty was engaged to be married, her heart was still in mourning. When Katharine had been nineteen and a college coed, Danny McCandless had been twenty-four and a cool-headed criminal. In her innocence, Katharine never thought that Danny might be bad for her. Now, ten years later, the shock of Danny's death lingered—but it was nothing compared with the rude shock of seeing him again.

### #375 DAY DREAMER by Karen Toller Whittenburg

At first Jessica Day thought she had just imagined him. But soon she realized that she could never have imagined anything half so strange and wonderful as Professor Kale Warner and his oddball tale of stolen research and cloak-and-dagger antics. And, even as Jessie was drawn into Kale's adventure, she wondered if someday she'd be left with only unbelievable daydreams of a man she could never forget.

### #376 MAGIC HOUR by Leigh Anne Williams

Oscar-winning director Sandy Baker wanted no partners on or off the set. But Victoria Moore couldn't help getting involved—her first and most autobiographical novel was being brought to the screen. Delving beneath the written word, the charismatic filmmaker uncovered Victoria's private sorrows and secrets. And despite the risks to her career and heart, Victoria couldn't suppress a burning need to know this man, this stranger, who understood her like a lover.

# Take 4 bestselling love stories FREE

## Plus get a FREE surprise gift!

---

## Special Limited-time Offer

**Harlequin Reader Service®**

Mail to

In the U.S.
3010 Walden Avenue
P.O. Box 1867
Buffalo, N.Y. 14269-1867

In Canada
P.O. Box 609
Fort Erie, Ontario
L2A 5X3

**YES!** Please send me 4 free Harlequin American Romance® novels and my free surprise gift. Then send me 4 brand-new novels every month, which I will receive months before they appear in bookstores. Bill me at the low price of $2.74* each—a savings of 21¢ apiece off cover prices. There are no shipping, handling or other hidden costs. I understand that accepting the books and gift places me under no obligation ever to buy any books. I can always return a shipment and cancel at any time. Even if I never buy another book from Harlequin, the 4 free books and the surprise gift are mine to keep forever.

*Offer slightly different in Canada—$2.74 per book plus 49¢ per shipment for delivery. Sales tax applicable in N.Y.

354 BPA 2AM9 (CAN)

154 BPA NBJG (US)

---

Name _____ (PLEASE PRINT)

Address _____ Apt. No. _____

City _____ State/Prov. _____ Zip/Postal Code _____

This offer is limited to one order per household and not valid to present Harlequin American Romance® subscribers. Terms and prices are subject to change.

© 1990 Harlequin Enterprises Limited

**Harlequin Superromance**®

A powerful restaurant conglomerate that draws the best and brightest to its executive ranks. Now almost eighty years old, Vanessa Hamilton, the founder of Hamilton House, must choose a successor.
Who will it be?

*Matt Logan*: He's always been the company man, the quintessential team player. But tragedy in his daughter's life and a passionate love affair made him make some hard choices....

*Paula Steele*: Thoroughly accomplished, with a sharp mind, perfect breeding and looks to die for, Paula thrives on challenges and wants to have it all...
but is this right for her?

*Grady O'Connor*: Working for Hamilton House was his salvation after Vietnam. The war had messed him up but good and had killed his storybook marriage. He's been given a second chance—only he doesn't know what the hell he's supposed to do with it....

Harlequin Superromance invites you to enjoy Barbara Kaye's dramatic and emotionally resonant miniseries about mature men and women making life-changing decisions. Don't miss:

- CHOICE OF A LIFETIME—a July 1990 release.
  - CHALLENGE OF A LIFETIME
    —a December 1990 release.
- CHANCE OF A LIFETIME—an April 1991 release.

# *Harlequin Superromance*®

## THEY'RE A BREED APART

The men and women of the Canadian prairies are slow to give their friendship or their love. On the prairies, such gifts can never be recalled. Friendships between families last for generations. And love, once lit, burns hot and pure and bright for a lifetime.

In honor of this special breed of men and women, Harlequin Superromance® presents:

**SAGEBRUSH AND SUNSHINE**
(Available in October)

and

**MAGIC AND MOONBEAMS**
(Available in December)

two books by Margot Dalton, featuring the Lyndons and the Burmans, prairie families joined for generations by friendship, then nearly torn apart by love.

Look for SUNSHINE in October and MOONBEAMS in December, coming to you from Harlequin.

MAG-01R